# Courage to Run

## A STORY BASED ON THE
## LIFE OF HARRIET TUBMAN

DAUGHTERS OF THE FAITH SERIES

# Courage to Run

## A STORY BASED ON THE
## LIFE OF HARRIET TUBMAN

*Wendy Lawton*

**MOODY PRESS**

CHICAGO

*For Rae Lynn,*
*a daughter of rare courage*
*who lost everything except her faith*
*before coming home to her new family.*

# Contents

# 1
# How Long, O Lord?

"Araminta Ross!"

Minty heard Annie's call, but the young girl's toes just wiggled deeper into the warm dirt as she sat partially hidden by the drying bush. A slender snake slowly zigged its way toward the fields, enticed out of winter hibernation by the balmy morning. The buzz of insects announced that the cold spell was over. Minty hugged her brown knees as she lifted her face to the warmth and opened her mouth as if to invite the sunshine deep inside.

"Minty, you ain't foolin' Annie. Git yourself in here and tend to these little'uns." The timeworn woman punctuated her words with the sound of a willow *switch* whipping against the door frame of the cabin.

It didn't take much for Minty to imagine the feel of that *switch* against the back of her legs. The old slave woman rarely used it, but it was long remembered by the children.

"Comin'." Minty jumped up and tried to brush the dirt

off her rough linen *shift*. She gave up. It was so soiled already, a little more dirt hardly mattered. "I'm comin' fast as I can, Annie."

"You help git these babies fed, or Annie'll teach you some sense."

Annie talked tough, but Minty already knew that most of it was bluster. Annie loved her babies, including the grown ones like Minty.

A trough half full of cornmeal mush was placed on the hard-packed dirt floor and children toddled toward it from all sides of the cramped cabin. Minty handed pieces of mussel shells to those children who were old enough to use them as utensils. The littlest ones used their fingers and managed to find their mouths most of the time. Children weren't issued clothing until they were almost ready to work, so cleanup was always easy.

❧     ❧     ❧     ❧

Minty was born a slave on a plantation near Bucktown in Tidewater, Maryland. Her *basket name*, given to her on the day of her birth six or seven years ago, was Araminta, but everyone called her Minty. When full grown, she would be called by her mother's given name—Harriet. Her mother never used the name Harriet. She went by Old Rit, even to her children most of the time. Minty didn't see why she couldn't have Harriet now since Old Rit never used it. Her mother just laughed when she asked, and told her, "Be patient, honey-girl. By 'n' by. Jes' be patient."

Minty hated those words. They were her mother's answer

to everything. How could she be patient when she longed to jump and run and grow up all at the same time?

Minty's father, Ben, and Old Rit were slaves on the same plantation, owned by Edward Brodas. Most of the slaves on the Brodas Plantation lived in the Quarter—a collection of ramshackle cabins located in a dirt clearing between the barn and the fields.

Minty loved the closeness of the cabins and the way it made all the slaves in the Quarter sort of feel like family. Minty's cabin was like all the others—rough-hewn timber walls chinked with mud, covered by a sagging roof. Inside was a single room with a packed dirt floor. A *wattle and daub* fireplace stood against one end. There were no partitions or windows. The dark, smoky room was home to Minty's entire family. Piles of worn quilts and scratchy blankets lined the walls and served as the only furnishings, but most of the living was done outdoors anyway. In one corner, a deep hole had been dug out of the floor. An old board covered the opening. Rit's hoard of sweet potatoes stayed cool long after harvest in this potato hole.

A broken piece of mirror was fastened to the wall near the door by two bent nails. It was too high for Minty, but every now and then Ben would lift her up so she could see. Wasn't much to see. She was small for her age, but sturdy. "Built like a bantam rooster," Ben used to say. Minty liked that. Those bantys were tough little birds. She laughed at the thought of herself hopping around the yard, scrapping for corn.

Old Rit worked in the Brodas house all day, helping the Missus. Ben worked in the woods cutting timber.

"Didn't used to cut so much timber," Ben said one day

after work, "but times been settling hard on the Brodas Plantation lately."

Many nights Minty pretended to be asleep and listened to her parents' whispered conversations.

"Started on a new stand today, Rit," her father whispered, talking about a new grove of trees he was to cut down.

"What'll he do when the timber runs out?" Rit asked.

Minty could always tell when her mother was worried because she'd rub her thumb and finger together real fast-like. Her rough hands made a sound like someone was sanding wood. That sandpapery rhythm often lasted long into the night.

"Tobaccy's bad these days. Not much call for cotton, or wheat neither," Ben whispered. "Just 'smornin' I heard the field hands marking time with a singin' of 'Poor Massa.'"

"Master Brodas best not catch wind of it," Rit said. The rubbing sound got faster. Minty knew the words of the song:

> Poor Massa, so they say;
> Down in the heel, so they say;
> Not one shilling, so they say;
> God Almighty bless you, so they say.

Rit slowly sucked air between her teeth—a sound that meant trouble was brewing. "Been noticing things lookin' pretty shabby 'round the Big House. Don't look like Master's growing enough of anything to keep the place goin'."

"Seems Master's mostly raisin' colored folk these days for hirin' out or worse," Ben said.

Minty knew what her father meant by "worse." Each time

the slave trader came to nearby Cambridge, Master rode into town. Since the invention of the cotton gin, plantations down South couldn't seem to get enough slaves. Congress halted the slave trade in 1808, so no more slave ships could land, bringing newly captured slaves from Africa. The only way to get more slaves was to buy them from other plantations.

Each time Master returned, Minty's stomach ached and she couldn't get a bite of food to go down. She waited for the sorrowing to begin. It didn't take long. Screams and cries erupted throughout the Quarter as families were told that one of their own had been "sold South." Late into the night, groups of slaves huddled together to sing in mournful tones:

> This time tomorrow night,
> Where will I be?
> I'll be gone, gone, gone,
> Down to Tennessee.

Sometimes they recited Scripture in unison: "The Lord is my Shepherd . . ." When the reciting finished, a lone voice broke the silence:

> Swing low, sweet chariot,
> Comin' for to carry me home.

Other voices joined in to swell the song:

> Swing low, sweet chariot,
> Comin' for to carry me home.

When all the folk were sung out, the night hushed. Even the crickets, whippoorwills, and hoot owls quieted. Slaves made their way back to their cabins, and long into the night you could hear the *keening*, weeping sounds of those who knew they'd never set eyes on their loved ones again.

Minty's own family still sorrowed. She had ten brothers and sisters, but just before harvest last year, two of Minty's sisters were sold South. Never would the young girl forget the picture of her sisters, chained by neck and leg shackles to a *coffle*—a chain gang of slaves—gathered from other plantations. The slave driver kept snapping his rawhide whip toward the *coffle* so that none of the slaves dared linger. Tears silently streaked her sisters' dusty faces.

Minty sat atop a fence post and watched them until she could no longer even see the dust from their trail. She continued her vigil for hours longer, squinting into the sun. Her stomach ached for days afterward. At night she listened to her mother rock back and forth on the floor, crying and praying, "How long, O Lord? How long?"

 

Annie was too old to be sold. She was too old to work the fields, either, so Master set her to tending the children in the Quarter. Minty helped Annie by tending and feeding the little ones. After the children finished scooping up the last of the mush, Minty carried the tray back to the cookhouse. She loved the happy jumble of toddlers and babies in Annie's cabin, but oh, how she hated being cooped up indoors. Whenever she was in the cabin she felt jumpy—kind of like she couldn't breathe.

Today, she took the long way 'round, circling by the fields. She lingered as she watched the field slaves move to a throbbing rhythm hummed in time with the motion of their work. Sometimes the song was a call and a response—someone would sing one line and everybody else would answer. No matter what, it sounded beautiful to Minty's ears. Sometimes she almost imagined she could feel the deep hum through the soles of her feet.

"Hey, you. You, gal."

Minty's heart began to thump in her chest. It was the overseer. He was in charge of the plantation and answered directly to Master Brodas. This swaggering man with a sweaty, beet-red face carried a long, braided leather whip. Many times Minty had seen him slash it across the backs of slaves to speed up a task. Sometimes, for no reason, he got a funny look in his eyes and the corner of his mouth twitched. The slaves knew it meant he was itching to whip someone—anyone.

"Yes, suh?" Minty looked at the ground. You didn't dare look white folk directly in the eye, else they might think you too bold.

"How old are you, gal?"

"'Bout six or seven." Minty was never quite sure, since slaves didn't mark birthdays. Someone said she'd been born in 1820 or 1821.

"Whose child are you?"

"Old Rit and Ben."

"Hmmm." He shaded his eyes from the sun with his hand as he lowered his head and looked at her for a long minute. "Well, you git, now. You hear?"

He didn't have to tell Minty twice. She turned and ran

back to the dark safety of Annie's cabin. *Old Rit'll be mighty unhappy to hear 'bout the overseer takin' notice of me. Can't do no good to come under his calculatin' eye, that's for sure.*

# 2
## Go Down, Moses

Minty always waited until all the mothers picked up their children before she left. Today, one of the mothers didn't come. The setting sun was already beginning to color the sky and baby Nicey was still at Annie's.

"Somethin's wrong, Minty. That's for sure." Annie rocked faster. "Um, um, um."

"Where's Nicey's mother?" Minty asked.

"Um, um, um." Annie shook her head as she made the dire sound deep in her throat.

It was nearly dark when one of the young women came to get Nicey. "Don't do a body no good to get that ol' overseer riled," she said.

"Where's Ruby?" Annie asked. Ruby was Nicey's mother.

"We was hoeing 'round the corn shoots today and she chopped one of the plants off by mistake. Jes' chopped it off. Overseer started hollerin' and yellin'."

"Lawd, have mercy." Annie continued to rock almost as if it could keep trouble away if she rocked hard enough.

"Made her so nervous-like, she chopped off another one."

Minty picked up the baby and gave her a piece of rawhide to chew on since Nicey was cutting teeth. Minty knew what was coming next. She should have recognized that satisfied glint in the overseer's eye when she ran into him.

"Overseer picked up his whip and slashed the clothes right off her back."

"Um, um, um."

"When Ruby wouldn't get up, he hauled her over to that hickory tree and tied her hands 'round with a strip of rawhide and whupped her and whupped her and—"

"Um, um um." The chair creaked under Annie's furious rocking.

"She been cut down now and Old Rit is layin' pork grease on her back."

Minty had to get outside. The room felt too close. With Nicey on one hip, she walked 'round and 'round the yard. How she hated slavery. All her life she had heard stories like Ruby's.

"When I grow up, Nicey, I'm gonna be free." Minty didn't know how, but even if she had to fly like a bird, she'd be free. "Maybe I'll take you with me. You'd like to be free, wouldn't you, Baby?"

"That kind of talk gonna get you whupped, girl, just like Nicey's mama." The young woman, done telling about Ruby, came up behind Minty and took the baby from her arms. "You be careful, now, Minty-girl. Y'hear? You don't need to go talkin' crazy."

After saying good-bye to Annie, Minty headed over toward her cabin. The Quarter was quiet tonight, so she took the long way—weaving in and around the other cabins before going home to supper. Once she got home, she'd be indoors again. As she meandered, bits of hushed conversations punctuated the quiet. The smell of night-blooming jasmine was a welcome relief from the stench of the outhouses.

Minty caught the smell of supper cooking all around the Quarter. The house slaves usually ate the leftovers from Master's table, but most of the families cooked their own evening meal.

Slaves never got paid for their work, but they did get a ration of food and clothing. Master Brodas would see that each slave received a portion of the cornmeal ground from the year's crop. They got pickled herring and pork occasionally, usually just enough to flavor the food. Sometimes a little wheat flour was added to the ration. Each family was allowed a small plot of land they could use to grow vegetables. Old Rit grew sweet potatoes and collard greens, black-eyed peas, cabbage, turnips, and beets. The men trapped rabbit and possum regularly. Sometimes on Saturday afternoon they fished in Buckwater River, snagged oysters out of one of the oyster beds, or trapped crabs. Depending on the season, sometimes they had plenty to eat. In the winter, stores got low and Minty went to sleep with an almost-empty stomach many nights.

The clothing was made by the slaves from cloth woven and dyed on the plantation. Every field hand was given two changes of clothing each year and one pair of shoes. Older children got a *shift*, almost like a long shirt. Little children and babies could run naked, so they received no clothing.

When the family's clothing wore out, Old Rit was careful to save every scrap. The threadbare scraps were pieced into quilts and stuffed with cotton when she could get it, corn shucks when she couldn't. Torn pieces of clothing were made over for the children.

As Minty drew near their home, she knew it was time to go in. She heard the sandpapery fidgeting of her mother's fingers even before she stepped into the cabin. A piece of pork fat was sizzling in the iron kettle hanging from a hook in the fireplace. It smelled good and reminded Minty it had been a long time since the noon meal.

Two of her brothers and a sister were sitting on the quilts along the edge of the room, but most were out and about. Everyone managed to converge on the cabin right about suppertime. It was always dark in the smoky cabin, but tonight even the open door yielded no light since the sun had set and supper was late. Old Rit must have stayed with Ruby until her husband came home.

"Minty, I hear you walked 'round by the fields this afternoon and came under the overseer's eye."

Minty could tell that her mama was none too pleased.

"Last thing I wanted was for that man to see how you growin'." The rubbing sound stopped as Old Rit poured water from the bucket into the kettle. A cloud of steam rose from the first splashes of water on the hot iron. The water would have to come to a boil before the cornmeal could be thrown in.

Rit sat and pulled Minty down next to her. "I had hoped to have you working with me up at the Big House before that man got any ideas."

"I'd rather work in the field."

"Araminta Ross, you don't know what you be sayin'." Old Rit shook her head. "Fieldwork is hot and hard. If you got on at the Big House, the days are filled with work, but not the back-breakin' kind."

Minty knew fieldwork was hard. She heard talk about slaves, broken from the endless work, who had to be sold down South. Cotton and tobacco growers were so hungry for labor in the Deep South that they were willing to make do with the last few years of a slave's working life.

"I hate being cooped up inside, Mama." Minty wasn't telling her mother anything she didn't already know.

"Oh, child, I wish you'd throw off those notions. There's nothin' a body can do 'bout being a slave, but I want your life to be as good as we can make it. If I can't work you into the house—well, I don't want to speculate 'bout it." The fidgety finger rubbing started back up.

Minty said nothing.

"You mightn't be any bigger'n a sack of cornmeal, Araminta Ross, but you carry more stubbornness in that stiff back of yours than any slave on Brodas Plantation."

Minty knew her back was usually stiff out of fear, not stubbornness.

"You tell Annie I want you carryin' water to the field hands, startin' tomorrow. If you look busy-like, maybe that man leave you alone."

Her mama's worried voice sent a shiver over Minty.

That night after supper, Ben and William Henry, one of Minty's brothers, brought in the big washtub filled with water. Minty knew it meant the slaves would be gathering for a singing, even though it wasn't Sunday.

Annie told Minty that slaves used to have their church right out in the open with singing and shouting and praising the Lord. Slave owners were getting more and more suspicious of their slaves lately and didn't like seeing them get together, even for church.

"They be afraid slaves jes' gonna raise up and slay they own masters," Annie said as she rocked back and forth. "It ain't the church folk they need be worryin' about."

There was a hollow by the creek bottom past the stables that they called the praying ground. Here, on a Sunday, they could gather to sing, preach, and pray without fear of disturbing Master or his family. On other days, the Brodas's slaves often met in one of the cabins for a midweek meeting.

Master Brodas hadn't forbade church meetings as many other plantation owners had, but word traveled like wildfire from plantation to plantation and the Brodas's slaves thought it wise to keep their worshiping to themselves—just in case.

That's why the washtub was here. Folks gathered around the tub and the water caught their voices to keep the sound from carrying through the night air. Ben laughed one night after service as he and William Henry emptied the tub. "After this water's done absorbed all the words and songs offered tonight, must surely be living water like in the Good Book."

They didn't have a Bible in their services. Even if they had one, none of them could read it. Slaves were forbidden to learn to read and write. The Bible stories, the Psalms, and the gospel were passed on by telling and re-telling. Much of what Minty knew about God she learned from her father. And even more from the singing.

Old Rit once told her, "Listen to the songs that Master Brodas's people sing when they get together. They all be about winnin' wars and cryin' and moanin' about lost love." She snapped her fingers as if to dismiss those subjects. "Our songs kep' us climbin' up the mountain and crossin' the deep river. Singin' done carried us on this sorrowin' journey. It be the words of our music, Araminta, that turned us slave folk from those Africa gods carved out of wood and stone to a livin', breathin' Jesus."

It was time for the meeting to begin. Minty loved to see her father stand and start the song. His voice was low and rumbly. At night, when he sang to the children, Minty loved to lean against him and feel the vibration of his song. Tonight he stood. He never told the people what song he was going to sing; he just started out:

Go down, Moses.

Everyone joined in, singing in harmony:

Way down in Egypt-land.
Tell ol' Pharaoh
To let My people go.

There was a swell of feeling when they came to the line:

Oppressed so hard they could not stand . . .

The song went on for a long time, sometimes with a deep humming underneath the words, other times in full voice. When the song finally wound down, Ben began to preach. "Moses was sent by the Lord to free the Hebrew slaves."

Several voices were raised in agreement. "Yes, sir," said one man.

"Um-huh," said one of the women.

"We spend our days lookin' for our deliverer," Ben said, "but we can't be forgettin' that Moses had to come under the eye of ol' Pharaoh before he could help his people. Like my Araminta." He looked over at Minty. "Today, she come under the eye of the overseer."

Minty heard some mumbling and a "Lawd, have mercy."

Ben continued, "Me and Old Rit know how Moses' mother must have worried when Pharaoh's daughter pulled that basket out of the bulrushes, but we be trustin' in the Lord."

Minty could see William Henry making faces at her. He was laughing because Ben compared her to Moses. She knew it must have seemed a funny comparison, but she loved hearing her father entrust her to God. If only she could have the courage of Moses.

Her father preached on for a long time. Sometimes Minty was pulled in by his words, but most of the time she just listened to the musical rise and fall of his voice. The rhythm of her father's teaching and the softly mumbled responses of the believers soothed her like singing, making her feel as if they were all working together to worship God.

The meeting ended on a happy note when everyone stood up, pushed the quilts over to one side of the room, and began a *ring shout*. Ben was the singer and another man was the *sticker*.

The *sticker* grabbed his broom and upturned his wooden box so he could beat out the rhythm with the broom handle on the box. Two other men were the *basers*. The *basers* answered Ben's song and set the intricate hand-clapping rhythm. Once the beat and the song led off, the women and girls started to move in a circle, singing and shuffling their feet to the beat.

Minty knew they could have gone on with the *ring shout* for hours, but work came early, so they only did "Lay Down Body," and after several variations, they closed the meeting with prayer—praying especially for Nicey's mother, Ruby. Everyone hurried off to their own cabins after the amen.

Minty wondered if her arms might just pull right out of her body. They ached from the heavy pails of water she hauled from the springhouse out to the field hands. She wouldn't complain, though. She was working out of doors, not stuck inside a windowless cabin or shut up in the Big House. She wondered how many times she made the trip today after she lost count. She was glad that she was able to give dippers full of cool water to the hardworking slaves.

She couldn't help thinking about her father's preaching last night. Did Moses ever give water to the Hebrew slaves who worked for the Pharaoh? She knew Moses must have hated slavery as much as she did. She couldn't help wondering if she could ever be as bold as Moses. It made her happy to think about being brave, but she was only a girl and a scrawny one at that.

"Hey, you." It was the overseer.

"Yes, suh?"

"You Araminta Ross? Ben and Old Rit's child?"

"Yes, suh." She kept her head down, but managed to catch a glimpse of him out of the side of her eyes.

"Master wants to see you." The overseer was grinning in that dangerous way that made it hard for Minty to breathe.

She looked around to see if she could see her mother or father, but she knew Old Rit was off working in the Big House and Ben was out cutting trees.

"Just leave the bucket, gal," he said. "Someone else will have to carry water to the hands." He laughed. "Won't hurt them to go without for a few hours neither."

Minty headed toward the Big House, hoping she'd run into her mother before she had to face Master Brodas. Old Rit was nowhere to be seen, but the Master was in the yard talking to a man seated in his wagon.

"Here she is, Mr. Cook," he said.

"She looks a mite young, don't she, Brodas?" The man was looking her over with a skeptical look on his face.

"Look, Mr. Cook, you said you could only afford to hire a child. Minty's all I can afford to let go for that price. Take her or leave her."

Hire? Master was hiring her out?

"All right, I'll take her, but we better be able to get our work outta her." The man called Mr. Cook talked in a coarse way—different from Master Brodas. "Get in the wagon, girl."

"No!" Minty was frantic as she spoke to Master Brodas. "I'll work hard here, Master. Please let me stay with Old Rit and Ben."

The Master turned his back and started to walk away. The man called Mr. Cook reached down and yanked her up by one arm. She scraped her leg on the splintery boards of the wagon as he dragged her across, dumping her on the seat beside him.

"Please . . ." She stood up, trying to reach toward him for mercy.

The man yanked her arm to pull her back into the wagon. "Shut up, girl. Stop fussin' or I'll whup you till you can't do nothin'."

"Master Brodas," she yelled toward his back, "can I make my farewells to Mama?"

No answer.

"Please, Master, please . . ."

Mr. Cook made clucking sounds to the horses and flicked the reins. The wagon pulled out onto the dirt road leading away from the plantation. The muffled clip-clop of the horses' hooves sent puffs of dust into the air. Minty looked back, hoping for a glimpse of her family, but all she saw was the Big House—getting smaller and smaller as she moved away from everything she knew and everyone she loved.

## 3
# A Long Way from Home

*I* hired you a helper from Brodas." Mr. Cook pushed Minty into the house as he spoke to his wife. Minty had no idea how far they had driven or how long she'd been on the road. She felt numb, like in her dreams when she sensed a great danger coming and couldn't move a muscle.

"You paid good coin for that scrawny thing?" The woman's voice was shrill. She stood with her feet apart and her hands on her hips. "She better be able to learn or you'll take her right back to that old cheat, Brodas."

*If I don't learn, they'll send me back?* Minty recognized the first tiny flicker of hope.

Though the house was much bigger than the Ross cabin, the whole structure could have easily fit inside the parlor of the Big House. Minty suspected that the Cooks were not what the Brodas's people called "quality." At the Brodas Plantation, the Missus and all her friends smelled like jasmine or rosewater. They wore their hair in little corkscrew curls that bounced as they moved. Mrs. Cook's hair was sort of frizzled and matted, like *hanks* of shorn lambs' wool she had noticed piled on the front stoop of the house.

From the moment she stepped into the house, Minty could hardly breathe. Mrs. Cook had been *carding* wool and the room was thick with flying fibers. As if dismissing Minty from her mind, Mrs. Cook resumed her work. As the woman combed the fibers across the spiked *cards,* the air danced with lint. Minty sneezed. Every surface wore a coating of fine wool fuzz. Minty looked toward the kitchen and saw the same fluff on the stove and the soup kettle. She sneezed again.

"Don't think you can get out of work by playing sick, girl." The woman wore a sneer on her face. "You'll get used to the wool, but iffen you never do, it don't matter none. You'll do the work or you'll get used to the back of my hand."

"Ah-choo."

"You'll sleep in there." The woman pointed toward the kitchen. "There's a plank near the fireplace. You can lay yourself down on that. Since spring is nearly here we won't go building any fires for you, though you might get a little heat from the embers."

"Ah-choo."

"Don't she talk, Mr. Cook?" The woman looked at her husband.

"I heard her beggin' Brodas to say her good-byes to her mama, but after that all I heard was snivelin' and cryin'."

"Look smart, girl. You best put your stuff over by your plank," Mrs. Cook said.

"She ain't got no stuff," Mr. Cook said.

"What did we git ourselves into?" Mrs. Cook didn't seem

to be asking anyone in particular. "Get a bowl of stew since it's well past supper. I'm quitting since the sun is too low to see anything." This was to her husband. She turned toward Minty. "You didn't do no work today, so you don't get no food. Soon's Mr. Cook is finished, you can go to your plank for the night."

"Ah-choo."

"Tomorrow you'll take up the trade of weaving."

Minty felt rumbles of hunger in her stomach. She had worked hard carrying water the whole day long, but it wouldn't be the first time she went to bed hungry. Somehow, stew coated in wool fuzz didn't seem very appetizing anyway.

Long into the night Minty lay there. Her bed was a bare plank of wood wedged in between the fireplace and the wall. Without even a straw-stuffed ticking or mat, Minty couldn't settle in. Mrs. Cook left a threadbare wool blanket by the plank, but it was itchy and smelled of mildew. Minty wrapped it around her anyway, trying to ward off the cold. She scrunched down as far as she could until her feet could rest against the still-warm stones of the fireplace.

She'd never slept alone before. In the big Ross family there was always someone willing to pull quilts together into a comfy huddle. When your feet got too cold you just tucked them under a soundly sleeping sister.

Minty felt like she was not only breathing wool lint, but that it had settled on every part of her body. She could even feel the fuzz between her toes from trying to get warm on the fireplace. She wondered if her hair looked like old Annie's tight black curls flecked with white.

*I hate this place. I hate Mr. Cook.* Minty didn't even like the smell of the man. His body had an oily, sharp kind of odor. When he talked, sour breath filled the room. In fact, every time he opened his mouth you could see gaps where some teeth had fallen out.

*I hate Mrs. Cook too. She is the perfect wife for Mr. Cook,* Minty thought. With her mean, squinty face, she looked like what the people on the Brodas plantation called River Trash. Minty understood why Master Brodas undertook the business of hiring her to the Cooks outside by the wagon. Mr. Cook was not *quality*—not the kind of guest to be invited indoors. Meetings between planters—people of quality—were always held in the library. Mother often served the delicate refreshments.

Mother. *How I miss you.* She thought about what Old Rit would say if she could hear Minty's thoughts about the Cooks.

"You don't be talkin' 'bout those folks that way, girl." Minty could almost hear the clucking sound in her mama's voice. Then she imagined that Old Rit would add, "Don't you be forgettin', Minty, they be Jesus' children same as you."

*Oh, Mama. I'm sorry. I won't be forgettin'.* She couldn't let this place make her mean.

She lay still, listening to the night. The sounds were so different from the sounds Minty was used to back home. The Quarter got real quiet at night. Sometimes she could hear the soulful who-who-who of a mourning dove or a medley of mockingbird warbles. In the spring and summer the chorus of chirping crickets sang melody to the harmony of croaking bullfrogs. And always, for as long as she could remember, Minty would fall asleep to the rhythm of the slap-slap of water against the banks, punctuated by the plop of a frog jumping into the river. How could she sleep here where all she heard was the rustling sounds of sheep milling around the pasture? Each time she drifted toward sleep, a bleating lamb awakened her. It sounded like a lonely child looking for its mama—kind of like Minty felt.

She used the corner of the blanket to sop up her tears and wipe her nose. She wasn't about to soak her board and let the Cooks see that she cried. *I have to get home to Old Rit and Ben. Somehow, I just have to.*

She heard a deep snoring sound coming from the Cooks' sleeping room. The rumble sounded like that deep throaty note that started the most mournful of all Old Rit's songs. It began deep in her chest and seemed to roll around, resonating in her throat before breaking into a lament:

> Sometimes I feel like a motherless child,
> Sometimes I feel like a motherless child,
> Sometimes I feel like a motherless child,
> A long way from home, a long way from home.

Minty could almost hear her mother singing. The next verse would build:

> Sometimes I feel like I'm almost gone,
> Sometimes I feel like I'm almost gone,
> Sometimes I feel like I'm almost gone,
> A long way from home, a long way from home.

And when she had almost sung out, she would sing:

> Sometimes I feel like I ain't got no home,
> Sometimes I feel like I ain't got no home,
> Sometimes I feel like I ain't got no home,
> A long way from home, a long way from home.

But she would always end with the motherless child, all sad and deep and lonely. Old Rit had also been taken far away from her mother and her home. *She must have felt as lonely as I do right now.* Minty touched the worn calico patch on her *shift.* Her mother had sewn it to cover a tear in the fabric. Her fingers followed the neat stitches running along the edge. As she fingered this reminder of her mother, she finally felt herself falling toward sleep.

"Git up, girl." Minty woke to the cranky voice of Mrs. Cook kicking the sleeping plank. "We working folk ain't lying abed all day."

Minty scrambled off her bed and folded the blanket. She was tired—bone tired. Her muscles ached from the heavy buckets of water she had carried all day long yesterday. *Was that just yesterday?*

"There's a chunk of bread for you on the table after you wash up. The pump is over there." The woman pointed toward the sheep pen.

Minty washed up by the sheep trough. A rag hung on the

fence near the trough. *At least it's far enough away that the water isn't covered in lint.*

"You don't need to do for us 'cept to empty the slops bucket." Mrs. Cook stood in the kitchen doorway.

The slops bucket. At the Brodas plantation at least they called it a chamber pot. *Don't be silly. Doesn't matter what you call it, it's still disgusting.* If someone from Old Rit's family had to relieve himself during the night, he got up and went out to the privy. No chamber pots for someone to have to deal with in the morning.

*You stop, Araminta Ross. Being mean won't help you none.* Mama wouldn't like it one bit. Minty went in and took the slops bucket and headed out to the privy to dump it. At least this was an outdoor job and she could inhale without fuzz tickling her nose. Of course, maybe it was better to wait and inhale when the task was done.

She went to the pump to rinse the bucket and wash up again before going inside. Mr. Cook was nowhere to be seen and Mrs. Cook was out with the sheep. One didn't dare sit at the table without being told, so Minty stood next to it. She bowed her head to thank God, same as she did with her family every morning of her life. She tried to remember Old Rit's words. "Lord Jesus." She paused, just like her mother, savoring the sound of the name. "Thank You for bringin' us through the dark of another night. We be grateful that the Almighty seen fit to allow us to wake up to a new day." Minty came to the part that always gave her chills. "And that You did not allow the bed I lay on last night to become my cooling board, nor my blanket my *winding sheet.* Amen."

Minty imagined the scene—her lifeless body, wrapped in

the mildewed blanket, stretched out on that plank by the fire-place. She could picture her family and friends back in the Quarter, mourning when they heard the news. Master Brodas would be very sorry that he hired her out to the Cooks.

Minty ate her piece of bread and drank the buttermilk that sat next to it. She had never eaten alone before.

"Are you still filling your belly?" It was Mrs. Cook.

"I'm just finished, ma'am."

"Well, it's time you started earning your keep. If you're going to be any help to me, I've got a lot to learn you, but the shearers are coming to cut the sheep in a day or two. I'll need you outside to git them ready."

*Outside.* Minty heard the word and felt relief wash over her. How she dreaded being closeted into the gloomy room off the parlor that held the spinning wheel and the loom.

꒐꒐ꙮꙮ         ꙮꙮ         ꙮꙮ         ꙮꙮ

Minty stood to stretch her legs. The outside work that sounded so good early this morning had turned her stomach sour in the first few minutes. The rest of the day was pure tor-ture. Sitting on the three-legged stool made her legs go to sleep. She walked a few steps but the pinpricks of waking legs hurt. It felt like she was walking on sharp sand.

When Mrs. Cook showed her how to clean the sheep in preparation for shearing, Minty didn't know how she could stomach it. She had to tie the sheep to the rail of the pen and, with a bucket of water and a bristly brush, she scrubbed the tail end of the sheep to remove all the dung. She'd knock off the flies as she worked, but very often the area was covered in maggots. Twice she had to knock ticks off her arm.

She never thought she'd make it through the day. When Mrs. Cook called her to break for lunch, Minty spent the whole time scrubbing herself with lye soap. The thought of food—any food—made her stomach lurch.

She wanted to run—run far and fast. It didn't matter where. *No. That's not true. I want to go back to the Brodas Plantation. I want my mother and my father. I want to stay with old Annie. I want to curl up with my brothers and sisters at night.*

Never had Minty hated slavery more than she did at that moment, but she knew she didn't have the courage to do anything about it. She was scared and she was lonely. There wasn't a brave bone in her body.

Back home she often heard brave whispers in the Quarter. "I'm goin' to run, and if Master sets the patrollers onto me, I'll stand and I'll fight—I'll fight to the death afore I let them bring me back in chains."

Minty turned those defiant words over on her tongue. How she wanted to be brave, but words like those seemed foreign to her. Old Rit had called her stubborn, but Minty only saw weakness. *Maybe God just made me to give in and do whatever folks tell me to do,* she thought. What if someone wanted her to do something that was downright evil? *How can I learn to be brave?*

"Girl." It was Mrs. Cook. "Did you finish the sheep?"

"Yes, ma'am."

"Well, wash up and set the table for supper. You know anything 'bout waiting table?"

"No, ma'am."

The woman snorted her displeasure. She stood with her arms folded across her ample chest. She was covered in lint. With the sun behind her, all her edges seemed fuzzy. For one moment, Mrs. Cook looked as lost and unhappy as Minty. As she turned to go scrub herself clean, Minty wondered if the setting sun was playing tricks with her eyesight.

She cleared the dishes from the table and stacked them in the *scullery.* Her bowl of mutton stew was cold and a layer of fat congealed on the top. *Just as well,* she thought. *It will cover the stew and keep the lint out while I clean up. I'll scoop the lard off just before I eat.*

"Tomorrow I'll learn you how to *warp* the loom." Mrs. Cook came out dressed in her nightgown and cap. "After you wash up the supper things, just set the dishwater aside. It's too dark to go out to the yard and dump it."

Her mother would be happy to know that her daughter was to learn a valuable trade. If only Minty could be happy as well. She looked at the lint-shrouded room that held the loom. Would she be shut up in weavers' rooms for the rest of her life? She could barely catch her breath just thinking about it. A wave of dizziness swept over her and she had to hold on to the edge of the table.

She remembered Mrs. Cook's words when they first met. "She better be able to learn or you'll take her right back to that old cheat, Brodas."

*That's right,* she reminded herself. *If I don't learn, they'll send me back.*

## 4

# God's Goin' Trouble the Water

We're weaving a *twill* for this lot." Mrs. Cook stood in the door of the loom room with her hands on her hips. "I got the *warp* ends cut and bundled. You take care you don't get them tangled up as we *warp* the loom. I already got a whole day into that bundle." She paused and squinted at Minty. "You listening to me, girl?"

"Yes, ma'am." Minty didn't understand a single thing Mrs. Cook said. *What's a twill? What are warp ends?*

"If you tangle this bundle, you'll see the back of my hand."

"Yes, ma'am."

"Now, listen good. To make a *twill,* this here *weft* crosses over two *warp* yarns and under one. Each *pick* moves over one. Makes the cloth a diagonal weave." The woman drew out the word *diagonal* to make it sound important. "Understand?"

"Yes, ma'am." Minty didn't have any idea what Mrs. Cook

was talking about, but the young girl already knew that if she could just bide her time till a person stopped talking, she could mostly pick it up by watching. Didn't do any good to start asking questions. Most times white folks just got all worked up and kept repeating the same instructions, only louder. If you still didn't get it, they got frustrated and started whupping.

"These here are *harnesses* and them are the *heddles*."

Harnesses. *That must be that whole frame full of wires. Those wires must be what she calls "heddles."*. Minty understood.

"First we wrap the *warp* ends around this here *warp* beam and roll 'em up." The woman got down on her knees behind the loom. Minty did the same. Mrs. Cook handed the huge *hank* of threads to her. She held it while the woman began tying the threads, one at a time, to a wooden bar.

"Ah-choo."

It took a long time, and their movement seemed to stir up the lint in the room. By the time they were done, Minty's legs had gone to sleep.

"Here now, hold the bundle." Mrs. Cook began untying the *hank* and unwinding it. "Don't you go tangling it now or I'll learn you a thing or two. I'm fixing to wind the *warp* onto the beam. As I need more *warp,* you unwind it from the bundle."

Minty could see that she needed to untie the threads holding the bundle together as she unwound the coils. How could she do all that with only two hands? It was heavy.

"Gimme more slack, girl."

*What's slack?* Minty continued to try to untie the knots with her teeth as she unwound the bundle.

Mrs. Cook never looked up. She used a handle to turn the beam as she spread the threads evenly across the bar and wound them up. "Don't let it slump to the ground," she yelled. "Too much slack, stupid girl, too much slack."

Slack must mean how much yarn was waiting to be rolled up. Minty's arms ached and her mouth was filled with fuzz from cutting the ties with her teeth, but she managed to keep up. They repeated this routine until what seemed like miles and miles of yarn was evenly wound onto the *warp* beam.

"I'm going to get up some lunch for Mr. Cook. You thread these ends through the *heddles*. Since we're making a *twill*, we only need three *harnesses*." She wet the end of one *warp* thread in her mouth and used her fingers to draw it out to a point. "The first end goes through this here *heddle* in the first *harness*. That's the one closest to you. Poke the second through the second *harness* and the third through the third *harness*." She demonstrated wetting, pointing, and threading. "There. You just keep repeating it. Next thread goes through number one again and so on. You understand?"

"Yes, ma'am." Minty did this time.

Mrs. Cook left the room and Minty got back to work. *What a tedious job.* She could see that you had to watch to make sure that you didn't cross any *warp* threads over—each one must be taken in turn. When she was finally done, she went to find Mrs. Cook.

"Them red beans is for you," the woman said. "Take them outside to eat. Just don't go losing the bowl or the spoon."

Minty sat on a stump in the yard to eat the soupy beans. She was hungry and the food tasted good. Even better than food was the fresh air. Flies buzzed around her, abandoning the sheep for a chance to settle on red beans. Minty didn't mind. *I'd rather face pesky flies outdoors than flying lint inside the house.*

"You fixing to spend the whole afternoon lolling around, girl?" Mrs. Cook's voice drowned out the buzzing flies.

"No, ma'am."

Minty finished her last spoonful and moved toward the house, her toes dragging the dust with each measured step as if to linger a moment longer.

By late afternoon the loom was fully *warped*. Mrs. Cook pulled the ends through the *reed* and tied them to the bar below the loom. "This here's the cloth beam," she said as she pulled the *warp* threads to begin the first wind.

It didn't pull evenly. The second and third threads were stretched to near breaking. "Stop, ma'am."

"What do you mean, stop?" Mrs. Cook said, jarred out of her routine.

"Those two yarns—I mean, ends—seem like they're fixin' to break, ma'am."

Mrs. Cook came around to look. "You stupid girl!" she screamed. "You crossed the threads." The woman jerked her arm over the opposite shoulder and hit Minty full force with the back of her hand. The smack caught Minty on the cheek and sent her flying against the wall.

"I worked and worked the day long and all you done is eat my food and mess up things for me. I knew you was a mistake from the very beginning."

Minty didn't move. Her whole head hurt—the back, where it slammed the wall, and her cheek from Mrs. Cook's blow. Even her teeth hurt. The violent impact caused a snow-storm of lint in the room.

"Ah-choo." It hurt to sneeze. Tears pricked her eyes. *Don't cry. Don't cry. Think of something good. Anything.* She searched her imagination to come up with something good. *Maybe she'll decide I'm not worth my hire and take me back to Ben and Old Rit—Father and Mother.* At the thought of home, she couldn't stem the tears welling in her eyes.

"Don't you go bawling, you stupid, stubborn thing. You deserve that much and more. For causing me so much trouble, you'll get no supper tonight and that's for sure." Mrs. Cook cursed as she went on talking to herself and unwinding the two crossed ends.

As Minty slumped on the floor, stunned by the blow, she felt her face swelling until she could see her own cheek with-out looking down. The skin felt tight and hot. She looked up and saw the woman, shoulders hunched and teeth clenched. Minty knew it would only make Mrs. Cook angrier to point out that the two crossed ends were the ones the woman had done herself before lunch.

"You git outside and tend the sheep until bedtime."

Minty gladly escaped.

Each day was much like the day before. Minty hated be-ing cooped up inside. Mostly her days were spent winding yarn on the shuttle for Mrs. Cook. Minty worked quickly, making sure one was ready to replace the one emptied by weaving. She learned that the yarn had to be wound with just the right amount of tension so as not to stretch the fibers. She figured she must have been doing a good job since Mrs. Cook's insults had tapered off some.

Today, for the first time, she was to do the weaving herself. The shearers drove in at daybreak. Since Mrs. Cook planned to be out in the pasture with them for most of the day, she had hired another girl to cook and serve food to the workers. Though nobody thought to introduce them, Minty smiled and the girl winked back.

"You leave Sally be, y'hear, girl? She has work to do and don't need to be lolling around with the likes of you." Mrs. Cook grabbed Minty's arm and pulled her toward the loom.

Minty's head hurt. The swelling in her face had gone down nearly a week ago, but her cheek was still tender. Maybe her sleepless nights were catching up to her. By the time she cleaned the kitchen each night, the Cooks were already long asleep. Though every bone in her body ached and she longed for rest, as soon as she lay down, homesickness would wash over her. Sleep was long in coming.

"Will you stop wool-gathering and pay attention?" Mrs. Cook said. "You may have to sit at the edge of this here bench since you're so short. Sit down."

Minty perched on the very edge of the bench. She could reach the *treadles* with her feet, but it was a stretch to keep the *treadle* pressed, throw a *shot,* and then reach forward to grab the *reed* and beat in the *weft.* If she strained every muscle, she could stretch her body from *treadle* to *reed* to perform the operation.

"I guess you'll do, though I don't know why Mr. Cook

couldn't have gotten me a bigger girl." The woman sighed.
"Don't forget we are weaving a *twill*. That means the weave is
two-one-two-one-two-one all the way across. The next row
is one-two-one-two-one-two. Each row takes turns—that's
what makes the pattern." Mrs. Cook seemed impatient to get
outside. "You understand, girl?"

"Yes, ma'am." Minty had watched the weaving for several days and saw how the raising of the *harnesses* opened a different combination of *warp* threads that made the pattern.
Pressing the *treadles* raised the *harnesses*.

"See, we got these *harnesses* tied to the *treadles*. *Harness*
one and three are tied to *treadle* one and . . . oh, it don't matter. Just press *treadle* three, then *treadle* two, then *treadle* one.
Then go back and do three, two, and one again. Keep on just
like that." The woman scrunched her eyes, looking hard at
Minty. "Pay attention and don't you go making no mistakes."

Mrs. Cook went outside to join the shearers. Minty started to weave. She stretched her foot to press *treadle* three,
threw the *shot* through the *shed* and reached up to beat the *reed*
against the weaving Mrs. Cook did yesterday. From the
kitchen she could hear Sally singing:

Wade in the water, wade in the water, children,
Wade in the water, God's goin' trouble the water.

She pressed *treadle* two and threw the *shot* again. As she
beat the *shot*, she stopped to listen. It sounded so good to hear
spiritual singing. Her voice was lower than Sally's, so Minty
added her harmony to the chorus. As she glanced toward the
kitchen, she could see the smile on Sally's face. Minty's

headache eased with the singing. *Where was I?* She remembered that she wove two rows, so she pressed *treadle* three, threw the *shot,* and beat.

She continued the weaving—two, one, three, two, one, three, two, one—singing along with Sally and alternating each *pick.* She beat the *reed* in time with the music. The weaving grew on the loom.

When Mrs. Cook came inside and told Minty to help set dinner out for the men, she was stiff from sitting for so long and straining to reach *treadle* and *reed.* Her head throbbed and her eyes burned, but she managed to carry out big bowls of greens, fried marsh rabbit, baking-powder biscuits, gravy, and corn pudding. A makeshift table had been set up using an old door and sawhorses. The men and Mr. and Mrs. Cook sat on benches around the table.

When she came back into the house, Sally set a plate on the kitchen table for her. It was the best food Minty had seen in weeks but she was so achy and tired, she could barely raise the food to her mouth.

"Are you feelin' poorly, sister?" Sally's hand on her shoulder startled Minty.

"I never fell asleep middle of the day before."

"You need to eat, hard as that ol' woman be workin' you." Sally made a clucking noise. "And you just a little thing."

Hearing a kind word and feeling Sally's sympathetic touch was more than Minty could stand. Tears rolled down her face. She used the shoulder of her *shift* to swipe them off her face.

"You Old Rit's girl, from over the Brodas's place, ain't you?"

Minty nodded.

"I can git word to Old Rit that you doin' a fine job here. My man tell me that your mama been prayin' powerful for the Lord to bring you back home."

"She is?"

"Uh-huh. Ain't a body around don't know how much Old Rit trust in the Lord."

Minty knew that was true. Maybe—just maybe—she would see her family again. She stood up to help Sally clear the lunch, but Mrs. Cook came in.

"C'mon, girl. She can clear up." The woman tilted her head, indicating that she meant Sally. "I need to check the weaving before I go back out."

Minty followed her. Mrs. Cook looked carefully at the work, her fingers playing over the weave closest to the *reed* and then moving slowly back across her work of the morning. When she got back to the very beginning of the morning's work where it was starting to bend over the cloth wheel, the woman screamed.

"You stupid girl. Stupid, stupid girl!" She bolted out of the house and came charging back inside with a green willow *switch*. Minty had no idea what went wrong, but she had no doubt about the punishment. She heard the *switch* whistle through the air as Mrs. Cook rained blows across her arms and legs. The pain was so intense that Minty could not stifle her screams. With each blow, it became harder and harder to breathe, until she fell to the floor, curled into a ball, and covered her head with her arms. The *switch* continued to slice through the air and connect with Minty's flesh.

"Mrs. Cook!" It was her husband. "What are you thinking of? You kill that girl and I'll have to pay Brodas as much as you make in a year. Stop it. Stop it this instant!"

The woman dropped the *switch*. Minty scooted to the far corner of the room. The rage still burned in Mrs. Cook's face. Her jaw was clenched, her chest heaved, and she breathed like she'd been running.

"The stupid girl ruined a whole morning's work." She pointed to the second *pick* in the weaving Minty had done. Minty had forgotten to alternate her first and second row. Two rows were the same. "It will take twice as long to fix this here mess as to do it myself."

*If I don't learn, they'll send me back.* She hadn't meant to make a mistake, but would her mistake be the way to get back home?

"I'll get you a new girl." Mr. Cook was trying to pacify his furious wife. Minty felt a surge of hope until he said, "I'll take this one to help me run the lines. I'll work her like a man full-growed."

"I'm going out with the shearers. I don't want to be seeing that stupid girl again. You can feed her out by the sheep pen." Mrs. Cook started out the door. "See if you can get Sally hired. She can cook *and* help me weave."

When she left, Mr. Cook turned to Sally. "See that them welts get doctored. I don't aim to have Brodas accusin' me of damagin' his property." He turned to Minty. "You be ready first thing in the mornin' to work the river with me. I'll be puttin' your food over on that stump outside. Don't you be comin' inside to sleep until Mrs. Cook has gone to bed. And you better be up and out of here before she's awake, y'hear?"

"Yes, suh."

The Brodas Quarter and her family seemed farther away than ever.

## 5

# Wade in the Water

You get down into that water, girl." Mr. Cook pulled Minty toward the rushing stream.

"But I don't know nothin' 'bout swimmin', suh!" Minty's headache hadn't lessened, despite spending much of the night outdoors.

"Don't matter none. Water's movin' fast, but it only comes up waist high." The man looked hard at Minty, as if seeing her for the first time. "Hmm. You're not very big, are you?" He reached into his satchel and pulled out a length of rope. "Tie this around your waist, girl, and we'll have a look-see."

"Tie it 'round my waist?" Minty felt fear tighten its bands around her chest until she could barely breathe. Her hands shook as she fumbled to tie knots. She wasn't very good at tying since she'd never had much practice.

"Come here, you stubborn girl." He untied her feeble attempts and knotted the rope tightly around her waist. "Now, jump into the water."

"I c-can't swim."

"I know that. Y'think I'm stupid? Everyone knows that coloreds can't swim."

His notion made her forget her fear long enough to catch her breath. Did he really believe that? She thought of her father who could swim like an otter. *If I ever get back home, I'm goin' to have Ben teach me to swim. That'll show this mean old—*

"I said 'jump.' I'll haul you out with this rope if the river is too high."

Fear washed over Minty once again as she stood at the very edge of the bank. Her toes curled over the thick, cool mat of grass that ended abruptly at the river's edge. Looking into the water made her head throb until she felt dizzy. "It looks c-cold."

"'Course it's cold. Now jump!"

Minty tried to propel herself forward but every muscle in her body shrank away from the rushing water. Just when she thought she might faint, she felt herself being launched toward the water. She'd been pushed. Hard. As her feet skidded off the grass they scraped against roots and shards of rock on the steep riverbank.

Too late, she realized that had she jumped, she would have hit the water feetfirst. As it was, she belly flopped into the rushing current. Water shot into her ears, mouth, and nose. A burning sensation hit her between her eyes, and her head felt as if it might explode.

The rope jerked against her waist and she realized that the current carried her to the end of her rope. She fought to lift her head out of the water—to gulp some air—but she ended up swallowing water.

*Jesus, help me. Help me now!*

"Stop that thrashin' around, you stupid thing, and put your feet down." From far off she could hear the voice of Mr. Cook. "Stand up, stand up!"

Minty realized that panic was making matters worse. *Jesus, calm Your child.* She remembered Old Rit praying this prayer over Minty when she became fearful. Her foot caught a bent root on the river bottom. As her other foot found the rocky bed, she stood up and managed to lean her head back and sputter and cough in the air.

Her nose and her head burned with every breath. Her teeth ached from the cold, but she knew God had worked a miracle. Oh, not a big Moses-type miracle like parting the water, but big enough for Minty.

The water came up to her neck, but she could breathe again. She remembered what Old Rit used to say to her. "Jes' remember, child—sometimes the Lord calms the storm, but most times He jes' lets the storm rage and calms His child." *Thank You, Jesus.*

"You done fightin' the river?"

"Yes, suh."

"Then I'll haul you out. Hang on to the rope with both hands."

Minty grasped the rope and felt her body being pulled back against the current. Water splashed into her mouth but, with the paralyzing fear gone, she kept her head above water for much of the time. As she got to the bank near Mr. Cook, he didn't let up. Instead of helping her climb up the bank, he yanked her over rocks and roots, branches and cattails.

"That were a fine performance." His lips curled into a sneer. "I've got half a mind to throw you back in."

Minty couldn't move. She lay on the cool grass, where she landed when the tugging on the rope finally stopped. Her head throbbed. Cuts and scrapes covered her arms and legs. Her throat hurt all the way to her ears.

"Don't think you can laze around all mornin', girl. We got us work to do." He kicked her side lightly with his boot. "Get that rope off. I'll need it to make a towline for you."

Minty's fingers were so cold and her shivers so violent, she couldn't unknot the rope. Mr. Cook jerked her to her feet and untied the rope.

"Gonna have you run my trapline for me. Won't have to do too much work. I just need to know when one of them muskrats is trapped so I can get it out and reset the trap."

"Muskrats?"

"Don't play stupid with me. You know about muskrats. Good eatin', that's for sure."

"Eating?"

"Called marsh rabbit. It's mighty tasty fried up like chicken." He was talking as he dug in his bag for more rope. "Real reason we trap muskrat is for the skins. Valuable skins. Got a beautiful warm fur, them muskrats."

He took off his boots, rolled up his pant legs, and slid down into the river, coils of rope over his shoulders. Minty's teeth chattered as she watched him. She had no idea what he was doing but as long as he didn't say anything she would try to blend into the brush.

☙ ☙ ☙ ☙

"Girl. You layin' there sleepin' whilst I'm doin' all the work?" He kicked her with his boot. "Get up."

"Yes, suh." The words came out raspy. Minty's head felt as if it were stuffed with cotton. As she stood, she swayed with dizziness. Something was wrong. She had never felt this sick before; never had an achy head that lasted overnight.

"This'll be easy now. I've tied a rope along the whole trapline." He pointed up and down the stream. "All you have to do is wade in the water, holdin' on to the rope, and check my traps."

"What do I check them for?"

"For muskrats, what do y'think?" The sneer was back in his voice. "I'll come by four or five times every day. You tell me where the muskrats are trapped and I'll collect them and reset the traps." He was unpacking traps. "I may be able to run more traps iffen I'm not havin' to wade the line all day."

Wade in the water. It reminded Minty of Sally's song. *Wade in the water, wade in the water, children/Wade in the water, God's goin' trouble the water.* She thought about that last line. Was that a promise? Would God trouble this deep water she was treading? She knew Old Rit was praying. She would pray as well. *Lord, will You wade with me?*

"Muskrats live near the edge of the stream where the water is shallow. They like to eat water lilies, cattails, and bulrushes. I hide my traps near the openin' of their burrows. They got one openin' underwater and a push-up hole on the bank for gettin' air." Mr. Cook kicked at a mound under some branches. "It's easy to spot their burrows once you know what you're lookin' for."

"Yes, suh."

"Underwater, you'll be able to feel the burrow openin's with your toe. Muskrats is the cousin of the beaver. You always find a mess of branches by their hidey-holes." He paused. "Anyway, it don't matter none, since I set the traps where I know muskrats will find them."

"Yes, suh."

"All you got to do is wade the line, and when I come back, you tell me where the traps are sprung." He waited for an answer. "You understand this, girl?"

"Yes, suh."

"So get in the water."

Minty slid down the bank near the rope that was strung along the river, just under the water. The cold water felt good on her hot body. *How did my body get so hot? Last thing I remember was shiverin' on the grass.*

The shallow edge of the river was still up to Minty's chest but she managed to hook her arm over the rope and move along through the water with the rope against her armpit.

"It's dinnertime. I'm goin' back to eat with the missus. You keep on workin' the line and I'll bring you some water and somethin' to eat later on."

Minty found that she needed to move slowly so as not to stir up the silt on the bottom. She needed to be able to see the traps. She carefully made her way from one end of the trapline to the other. The sun beat down on her head and shoulders while her body shuddered in the icy-cold water.

She didn't know what was wrong, but she had never been this sick before. More than once she thought she might faint. *If I faint, will the cold water revive me as I slip under?*

The first time through, all the traps were empty. On her

return trip, she saw a disturbance and realized that a muskrat had been caught in the steel jaws of the trap. She looked closer. At first she felt repulsed—the muskrat looked too much like a rat. The thought that she had eaten fried muskrat made her stomach pitch.

The muskrat's tail slapped the water. It was flat. Not as big as a beaver's, but not a rat's tail either. His feet were almost webbed. He was caught by the skin and did not seem to be seriously injured.

"A curious critter you are, Muskrat," she rasped in a scratchy voice. "And how frightenin' to be caught in a trap."

*Not so different from me. Why should such things be? Animals caught in traps. People held captive as well.* Minty's headache was causing her vision to blur. *Is there no help for the muskrat? Is there no help for my people?*

"God's goin' trouble the water." *Did someone speak the words out loud?* Minty couldn't be sure. She looked around but no one was about.

*There may be no help for my people right now, but maybe there's help for Old Muskrat.* Minty held her breath and went underwater. She pulled at the trap, trying to free the muskrat, but she wasn't strong enough. She tried again. The muskrat became more agitated until he finally tugged himself loose, leaving a piece of his hide in the trap.

"It may hurt for a while, Old Muskrat, but freedom be worth the pain." *Yes, freedom is surely worth the pain.*

Minty waded the line one more time. She shivered violently and had trouble catching her breath. Mr. Cook still hadn't come back, but she knew she had to pull herself out of the water. As she crawled up the embankment, the wooliness in her head made her feel woozy. She had to make it onto the grassy bank, but her arms and legs were numb. *Old Rit, I need you. My head hurts and my throat hurts and my . . .*

"Get up, girl."

Minty could hear a voice from far off.

"How long you been layin' here?" A pause. "Well, I'll be jiggered. This here stubborn slave ain't worth the penny I paid that old cheat, Brodas. She don't help the missus with the weavin' and now, when I set her a simple task, why, she lays aside the river and takes a nap."

Someone was kicking her. *Annie? Is it time to feed the children? When will Old Rit get home? I need my mother. I don't feel well.*

"Get up, girl. Get up, y'hear?"

There was that voice again. *Who is it?* She felt herself being hauled up and slung over a man's shoulder. *Ben?* Her body was dropped onto something rough and hard. She hit with a thud, but one more ache hardly mattered.

"Mrs. Cook, somethin's wrong with this here girl. I'm dumpin' her out here by the pump, but you watch her now, y'hear? I don't want her dyin' and Old Brodas dunnin' us for money."

*That voice again. What was it saying?*

"Worthless slave ain't worth a plug nickel dead or alive." The man's voice blustered but Minty heard a quiver of fear as well. "That Brodas will hear me out this time iffen somethin' happens." Minty heard the man's steps walking away.

Minty heard herself moaning as hands roughly poked at her, but she couldn't stop the sound. She hurt. Every part of her body hurt.

From right next to her ear, a woman swore. "That wagon is from Brodas's Plantation." The voice moved away as it swelled to a shriek. "Sally, run git Mr. Cook. Tell 'im we got trouble on our hands."

The voice grew distant as warm blackness swallowed Minty.

# 6

## I Hear the Train A-Comin'

"Minty, baby. Can you hear your ol' mama?"

Minty knew she must be dreaming. She heard her mama's voice and she felt those beloved sandpapery fingers stroking her face. Her body ached but she could almost imagine she was cradled in her mother's arms. *Did I die? Do I rest in the arms of Jesus?* She put her hand to her achy chest. No, she could feel the scratchy river-crusted *tow-linen shift. No glory robes for me yet.*

"Honey-girl, wake up. It's Ol' Rit. Please, Minty, wake up."

Minty hated to leave the darkness. Nothing hurt back there, but as she began to fight her way toward Old Rit's voice, her eyes burned. Each breath made her chest ache. Her head throbbed as the rocking movement of a wagon jostled her.

"Mama?" The sound was more like the croak of a bull-frog.

Minty reached up and touched her mother's wet cheeks.

"Thank You, Lord. My baby's done come back. He'p me get her home, Lord Jesus, and jes' soothe her fever and ease her breath."

*Home.*

Minty caught one word from her mama's prayer. The word that conjured up the smoky haven of that cramped cabin in the Quarter, filled with the talking, laughing voices of her father and mother and sisters and brothers. Home.

"Minty, Mama's takin' you home."

The young girl felt her body go limp in her mother's arms as the thought of going home swallowed all the loneliness of the last weeks.

"You been pow'ful sick." Annie sat on an upturned crate beside the stack of quilts that made Minty's bed. "Master set one of the field hands to watch the little'uns so's ol' Annie could come watch over you."

"Thank you." It was half bark and half cough.

"They say Master feel bad 'bout you getting so sick over to that Cook place." Annie rocked back and forth on the crate and muttered that familiar old sound, "Um, um, um."

Annie communicated many different meanings by that one sound, yet Minty never misunderstood. The old woman's body lent the clues. When Annie's eyes widened and her body tensed as she mumbled the um-um-um, it meant trouble was brewing. The very sound raised goose bumps on Minty and made the hair at the nape of her neck feel shivery. Other times, when it came with a pursing of the lips and a slow shaking of the head, it announced distaste for someone's wild behavior—a kind of warning that no good would come out of evil. This time, however, Annie's eyes narrowed and an unspoken criticism rumbled in the um-um-um. It wordlessly declared what she thought about slave owners who hired out children to folk who didn't know how to take care of them.

"Old Rit says that Mrs. Cook's Sally got word to Ben that I was sick. My mama went straight to Master." Minty hoped to thank Sally someday.

"Master's conscience must'a finally grabbed hold'a him, since he let Cicero take the wagon and he'p your mama fetch you." Annie smiled. "I heared that ol' Mrs. Cook was so mad she wouldn't let them take you till Cicero gave her the piece of paper from Master."

Minty turned toward the door and saw Old Rit carrying Nicey. "You carried Nicey over here for a visit?" Minty loved Ruby's little baby.

Rit didn't answer and Minty could tell something was wrong.

"Minty's measles done run they course now," Annie said. "The lung fever is hangin' on, but ain't nobody can catch that."

Rit plopped the baby on the quilts next to Minty. Nicey seemed uncertain, almost as if she had forgotten Minty.

"Nicey, baby, it's me, Minty." Her voice was raspy and much deeper than it was when she left Brodas Plantation. The baby stuck her thumb in her mouth and looked at Minty with distrustful eyes. Minty reached out and poked the baby's tummy. Nicey pulled her thumb out of her mouth and put her arms out toward the girl in recognition.

Minty pulled Nicey on top of her. "So, now you be re-memberin', hm?"

"Can you tend the baby so I can talk to Annie?" Rit seemed worried.

Minty bounced the baby up and down, but since her illness, Minty tired easily, so when Nicey laid her head down on Minty's shoulder and stuck her thumb in her mouth, Minty was ready for the rest.

". . . knowed she done taken off. Got the patrollers out hunting." Minty could hear her mother whispering to Annie.

"We heared the bells clanging and then the dogs. Don't blame her none, that Ruby. She knowed Master was fixin' to put her on the block. That overseer been meaner and meaner to her. Reckon he took a notion to hurt a body and Ruby be the one he lay that evil eye on."

"Hush, Annie. Don't you go gettin' in trouble jes'cause you riled. Nicey goin' need you more'n ever."

Minty knew what they were talking about. Ruby must have heard that they were planning to sell her South and she ran off. She was taking a big chance. Most runaways were caught and dragged back in chains. They were whipped—given "nine and thirty"—and sometimes the thirty-nine lashings left them close to death. The letter R—for runaway—was also branded into their flesh.

They were often sold anyway, since the further south, the harder it was to make it to freedom. Slave owners knew that a slave who had tasted freedom, however brief, would most likely work up the courage to try again, no matter the cost. They didn't want that kind of influence in the Quarter.

"Didn't never think Ruby'd pluck up courage to run. Her

with Nicey. Ain't often mothers with sucklin' babies run. Um, um, um." Annie shook her head with admiration.

"Ruby knowed you love Nicey, Annie. She knowed the only way she ever see Nicey again is to get free and save the money to buy her child out of slavery." Rit sighed. "I don't hold none with runnin'. It be best to bide our time, but Ruby done the only thing she could."

"If I don't live long enough to see Nicey growed, will you tend her?"

"I give my word," Rit said. "I be prayin' she catch that train."

Nicey put her chubby hands on either side of Minty's face and rubbed faces, then gave Minty a wet kiss on the nose. They had both fallen asleep. The rag diaper tied around Nicey was sopping wet. Minty took Nicey's little hands and planted a kiss in each palm. She could hear Annie humming from outside the door. Since Annie came to care for Minty, they had become friends, despite the decades between them.

"Annie."

"Yes?"

"Nicey be awake and in need of a washin' off."

Annie came over and untied the soggy rag. She washed Nicey with water from the bucket and tied a fresh rag on the baby.

"Annie, what did my mother mean about Ruby catchin' a train?"

"Shush, child. You don't be talkin' 'bout no such thing." The old woman put her finger on her mouth and moved toward the door with Nicey in her arms. She stepped outside and Minty could hear Annie's sauntering steps on the soft dirt around the cabin. Must've looked like she was taking Nicey for a slow airing.

She came back inside and laid Nicey beside Minty.

"Your mama be talkin' 'bout the Underground Railroad," she whispered. "It more'n likely is a story made up, but patrollers say that some slaves jes' disappear, almost like they be an underground road. Not even the dogs can find 'em."

The story made Minty shiver. "Is it a railroad like the one that brings the Brodas's relations from the north?"

"No. Some folks think that when patrollers say 'underground road,' others heared it wrong and called it 'Underground Railroad.'" The old woman lowered her voice again. "Nobody knows for sure, but some folk jes' don't get caught and they jes' don't come back."

"If only they could come back and tell us how to find the road," Minty said.

"Once a body be free, ain't never goin' come back to slavery, child. Ain't never."

"Slavery just don't make any sense, Annie." Minty had been thinking about this. "It surely is bad, and not just for the slaves. When I lived over at the Cook place, I noticed that learnin' how to look down on folk ruined them. Do you think that whippin' people turns white folk mean?"

"Maybe. All white folk ain't mean. I heared that some white folk up north are workin' to get slaves free."

"I wish I could be free. My whole family too. Free."

"Won't be happenin' less'n you make it happen, Minty."

"I know. But I'm all the time scared, Annie," Minty confessed. "I'm scared of everything. I keep askin' the Lord for courage, but my bones turn to corn mush when I come up against trouble."

"When my babies got sold away, long 'fore you was born, I got angry with God. Angry with myself, too, that I ain't had enough courage to fight for my babies."

"How did you get courage, Annie?" Minty knew Annie wasn't afraid of anything.

"I finally seen that the Lord loved me like I loved my babies. Courage growed when I had nothing more for white folk to take. Most important person to me can't never be taken away." Annie laughed. "That'll stiffen you for the fight."

"The most important person?"

"Lord Jesus." The old woman was matter-of-fact. "You jes' keep on prayin', girl. God don't seem to waste courage when you ain't needin' it. He sorta saves it up for when you need a dose."

"You be sayin' to trust that courage'll be there, even when you can't try it out beforehand?"

"Uh-huh, like Moses. He done beg the Lord to pick anybody 'sides him for the job of leadin' the slaves outta Egyptland. You know what God say?"

"Go down, Moses."

"Uh-huh. That's what he say." Annie picked up the baby and took her outside. Minty meant to think about everything Annie had said, but she felt her eyes getting heavy.

Minty had been back at the Brodas Plantation for several weeks. Her measles had only lasted a couple of weeks, but the lung fever hung on. Minty's voice was lower and raspier and most of the folk believed the change most likely permanent.

Ben laughed when she sang, telling her that her new voice was like no other. It had a deepness that was surprising in a young girl. When she joined the singing, her voice added a resonance that folk commented on.

Minty was helping Annie with the babies again. She spent her days with Nicey on one hip and a line of toddlers following her wherever she went.

"Minty."

It was Old Rit calling her. What was her mama doing in the Quarter in the middle of the day? Something must be wrong. Minty picked Nicey up off the ground and ran toward Annie's cabin, a passel of children toddling and tumbling after her.

"Master called to me this mornin'." Old Rit was rubbing her fingers together, though she tried to sound matter-of-fact. "He declared you was well enough to go back and finish your hire with the Cooks." Old Rit sat on a crate near Annie's rocking chair and put her arms around Minty and Nicey. "James Cook been pesterin' Master Brodas about either getting you back or getting his coin back."

"Back?" Minty couldn't believe the words her mother was saying. "I thought I was home to stay!"

"I been hopin', but . . ." Old Rit couldn't finish her words.

"Rit, them folk ain't fit to hire Minty." Annie said her piece.

"We don't have no say-so, Annie. Mr. Cook is comin' to fetch my baby."

Nicey put baby hands on Minty's face and gave her one of those smeary kisses. Minty pulled away from Old Rit. She felt betrayed even though she knew her mother could do nothing.

"Honey-girl, you try real hard to learn the weavin'. I want you to have a trade so's you won't spend your days laborin' in the hot sun like livestock."

Minty didn't answer. She felt as if she were back in that stifling room with lint floating in the air. She could barely catch her breath.

"Ah-choo."

"Are you sick, Minty?" her mother was rubbing rough fingers over her face. Nicey could feel the tension and began whimpering when Annie took her from Minty.

"No," said Minty, squaring her back. "I hate weavin' and I hate bein' indoors."

The overseer called from the yard. "James Cook is here with his wagon. He's come to carry 'Minta over to the Cook place. Where is that girl of yours, Rit?"

"She coming, sir." Rit put her arms around Minty and whispered, "I love you, baby. Lord Jesus keep her safe." The woman kissed both of the girl's palms and said, "You jes' be patient, Minty, by 'n' by."

Minty walked outside.

"Courage, Minty," whispered Annie.

Courage. Maybe courage was just putting one foot in front of the other and not thinking too far ahead.

*If I don't learn, they'll send me back.* Minty walked over to the wagon and crawled up onto the tongue and into the back. She sat down, leaning against a bale of wool in the bed of the wagon. This time she said her good-byes, waving to the sorrowing huddle of slaves—Old Rit, Annie, Nicey, and the babies—until the wagon turned the bend.

# 7
## 'Buked and Scorned

If Minty thought that her last stay at the Cooks' house was bad, this time was worse. One day just ran into the other and one season ran into the next, interrupted only by punishments handed out by Mrs. Cook. Minty shivered through winter and sweated through summer.

She stubbornly refused to learn the different weaving tasks. When she failed, she was punished and sent outdoors. Each time the door shut behind her, she filled her lungs with lint-free air. The sun, the rain, the breeze—all were a balm to Minty.

That wasn't the only reason she wouldn't try. Minty knew if she learned to help Mrs. Cook, the Cooks would let Sally go and keep Minty on. She was as cheap an apprentice as they could get, but Minty understood how much her friend Sally needed the indoor job.

Spending time with Sally helped ease the homesickness. Sally relayed messages from Brodas Plantation to Minty and carried the lonely girl's words back. Minty's time away from her family was still difficult, but as Sally often reminded her, "Just be glad you ain't been sold away. You just hired out for a time." Minty tried to be content with that.

Mrs. Cook shook Minty awake early one morning. "Git up and gather your things. Your hire is over with us."

"I'm leaving?" Minty wondered if she was dreaming. Sometimes her dreams were more vivid than her waking hours.

"That old cheat, Brodas, was fixing to charge more on your rehire since you're two years older'n when we first hired you." She sniffed. "Mr. Cook told him you was worthless two years ago when we hired you and you're still worthless."

Minty remembered those long-ago words of Mrs. Cook, "She better be able to learn or you'll take her right back."

Was she finally going back to her family for good? Minty folded her quilt. How happy she had been the day Sally brought it to her. Old Rit made it from scraps of old clothing. Minty pretended she could catch the smell of pitch on the pieces from Papa's overalls and the faint odor of cooking from the red patch made from her mother's worn headcloth. When she wrapped her quilt around her it was like being hugged by her family. Her family. Would she be seeing them this very day?

She said her good-byes to Sally and sat on the stump by the sheep pen to wait.

Minty soon saw the dust cloud raised by the wagon wheels on the dirt road. Putting her hand over her eyes, she strained to see who was driving. As it came into view, she saw Cicero with Old Rit sitting beside him.

"Mama!" Minty didn't wait for the wagon to pull into the yard. She ran.

Her mama didn't wait either. She jumped down before Cicero even stopped the wagon. "Minty, baby. How you growed! I 'most didn't recognize you."

Old Rit looked exactly the same to Minty. Beautiful. Never had anyone looked so beautiful to her. When her mother's arms wrapped around the young girl, it felt like home.

"How did you get leave to come fetch me?" Minty knew the Missus did not care to be without her cook, even for a few hours.

"I asked for leave to see my baby. Been too long since I laid eyes on you." Old Rit took the quilt out of Araminta's arms. "I see you got my quilt."

"Yes. When Sally brought it to me, it felt like family. I found Papa's overalls, William Henry's breeches, your head-cloth. I even thought this piece of calico might be the pocket from Annie's apron."

"That's right. When Annie found out I was making it for you, she unpicked the threads holding the pocket. Said a body could do with one pocket on such a fine apron, 'stead of two."

Minty knew the sacrifice that represented. That apron was one of Annie's prized possessions.

"And the back of the quilt was made out of Nicey's old diapers. I soaked 'em in bluin' and cut away the worn parts."

"Nicey's too big for diapers now?" Minty couldn't wait to see her little friend.

"Want to know how I got the wool to stuff it?" Old Rit was grinning. "Your Papa had Sally's man trade some of my sweet 'taters to Mrs. Cook for a bundle of her wool. Ben thought it a fine joke that the wool from those stingy folks be warmin' our little girl after all."

Minty laughed at Papa's joke. She had often caught Mrs. Cook eying the quilt as it lay carefully folded on Minty's plank. Nobody pieced a quilt as fine as Old Rit. The colors and the pattern made a stunning design.

Cicero reached down to give Minty a hand up. Old Rit climbed up and sat beside her. Nobody came out to say any good-byes, so Cicero giddyupped the team and turned around the yard and headed back out the road.

"I can't hardly bear to wait to see everyone."

Minty heard the fidgeting of her mother's fingers long before she understood something was wrong.

"Honey-girl, that's why Master let your old mama come see you. You're just goin' have to be patient some more. Master Brodas done hired you out again. I know you'll be home by 'n' by, but—"

"I'm not goin' home?" The lightness dancing in her chest since morning sank into a hot, painful knot in her stomach. She had trouble pulling the next breath into her leaden body.

"No, Minty, baby." Old Rit put her arms around the girl. "Plantation's still troubled. Master's been hirin' out more slaves every year. The Quarter's gettin' quieter and quieter."

Minty couldn't get a single word past her throat. *I hate slavery. A body doesn't have a say 'bout anythin'. People do whatever they want with you. Master worries more 'bout his huntin' hounds than he does 'bout his slaves.*

"Minty, you be hearin' me?" Old Rit must've been talking. "You be going to a young couple with a new baby. They want a maid-of-all-work and a nursemaid. Master Brodas recalled you carryin' Nicey ever'where you went and thought it'd be better'n hirin' you another year to Cooks."

Minty murmured an acknowledgement.

"It be good inside work. I don't never intend watching you get your brains fried workin' in the field year after year. I always hoped to see my girls workin' as house slaves." Old Rit got quiet.

Minty wondered if her mother was thinking of the two girls that had been sold South. Not much chance they'd ever get word of them, but if they were still alive, they were most likely working the cotton fields.

"I know, Mama. I'll do my best." Minty took the quilt and folded it onto her lap. *'Least I'm luckier than Joseph from the Bible. He got sold into slavery, but not before his brothers took away the patchwork coat his papa gave him. I still have my quilt.*

The horses trudged on, their hooves making a rhythmic thudding in time to the sad tune sung by Old Rit and Cicero:

> I've been 'buked and I've been scorned,
> I've been 'buked and I've been scorned,
> I've been 'buked and I've been scorned,
> I've been talked about, sure you born.

Minty loved to hear the singing, even if she didn't feel like joining in. They got to the last verse:

> Ain't gwine lay my 'ligion done,
> Ain't gwine lay my 'ligion done,
> Ain't gwine lay my 'ligion done,
> I've been talked about, sure you born.

Minty stiffened her back. Many of her people knew the secret: with Jesus, a body could bear almost anything. And when you couldn't bear it any longer, Jesus carried you home in His gentle arms. Ben used to say that the Lord Jesus wept right along with them.

As the wagon pulled up in front of the freshly white-washed frame house, Minty reminded herself that she wasn't only bringing her quilt—she had Jesus with her as well.

How hard it had been to say good-bye to Old Rit. Cicero took the wagon around back and knocked on the back door. A pretty young woman answered the door.

"Miss Susan?" When Cicero saw the woman incline her head slightly he continued, "I carried your new girl over from the Cooks' place. This here be Araminta Ross from Brodas Plantation." Cicero pushed Minty forward. "They call her Minty."

"Hmm." Miss Susan looked Minty over. "You are the one that Edward Brodas said was good with children?"

"Yes, ma'am."

"All right. Come in, come in." She flicked her hand toward Cicero. "Get on home, boy. I'm sure Edward Brodas does not feed you in order to have you standing idle here."

Before she stepped into the house, Minty turned around to get one last look at her mother sitting in the wagon. Cicero climbed up beside her and flicked the reins. *Seems like my life is just one good-bye after another.*

"Stop dawdling, girl. There's much work to be accomplished and I intend to get my fair share out of you."

Minty followed Miss Susan into the house. It was a fine house, filled with pretty things. The young woman led from the back door along the hallway and up a flight of wooden stairs.

"These are the back stairs, girl. I don't want to catch you traipsing up the front staircase, y'heah?" Miss Susan's voice was soft and fluttery, but Minty caught the ugly undertone. "Put your things here in my room, next to the baby's cradle."

The room held a bed, draped in linens, and a small draped table with sparkly bottles, jars, and a brush set atop it. An ornate mirror hung above the table and a draped stool in front of it. Two chests of drawers stood on either wall of the far corner. In the near corner was a highly polished cradle. Next to that was a rough-hewn trunk.

"You may put your things in that trunk. You will find another blanket in there. Since you already have a quilt, you may keep the blanket to wad up as a pillow. You are not infested with lice, are you?" Miss Susan stood with her arms bent at her waist and her hands resting one on the other. Her skirts were so wide from the hoops underneath that her arms could not hang down without popping the front of her hoop up.

"No, ma'am."

Miss Susan smelled of jasmine. Minty had never seen anyone dressed as fine as her new mistress.

"You'll find a *linsey-woolsey* dress in that trunk as well as three aprons. See that your aprons are always clean and starched. You'll have to do them up in your spare time. Sadie will find you a pair of shoes and stockings. I don't want you embarrassing me in front of my friends, y'heah?"

"Yes, ma'am."

"My sister came to stay over the past season to help with Baby Lucinda. Emily's room is down the hall. My husband's room is right next to mine, just through that door. You are never to bother him. Neither speak to him nor even raise your eyes to him, y'heah?"

"Yes, ma'am."

"I expect you to care for the baby. She's a fussy thing and cries much of the time. My husband expects me to be well rested, so you will have to rock her throughout the night when she stirs."

Minty wondered how she would wake in time to calm the baby.

"During the day, I expect you to wait table and do the light housework. I have a woman who comes in to do the heavy cleaning. Sadie is out in the summer kitchen and won't want anyone bothering her."

Miss Susan went on and on. Minty knew she was in for trouble. She couldn't possibly remember all the things being said. *Go here. Don't go there. Do this. Don't do that.*

"Are you listening to me, girl?"

"Yes, ma'am."

"Since my sister is still out with the baby, I want you to tidy up the parlor. Let me show you where to find the feather duster and the broom. I want the room finished in time for you to wash up, change into your clothes, and be ready to serve luncheon." Miss Susan talked slowly and formed her words carefully. Her voice sounded as sweet as the jasmine scent she wore, but she never stopped giving orders. Minty already noticed that her two favorite phrases were "I want . . ." and "I expect. . . ."

When Miss Susan was finally gone, Minty set to work. She had never been in such a fine room, let alone had to clean one. She took the feather duster and began whisking it around all the tabletops. Each surface was covered with pretty things—little boxes, wax flowers under glass domes, clocks, and other pieces Minty couldn't identify. There were cro-cheted doilies like the ones Annie sometimes made for the Big House.

Minty chased the dust around. Every time she looked back at the furniture already finished, she could see a fine coating of dust begin to settle once again. When she dusted the whole room, she took up the broom and began to sweep it across the carpet. The harder she swept with the bristly broom the more dust swirled into the air. Miss Susan was right, this room needed a good cleaning. Minty finally cor-ralled the dust in a pile near the door. Going back, she began to sweep the wooden floor around the carpet, scooting that pile into the pile from the carpet. The air was dancing with dust motes.

*There. I think I dusted and swept everything.*

At that moment the door swung open and a gust of wind swirled the pile of dust back into the room.

"Well, I never . . ." The words slipped over Miss Susan's lips like honey sliding over the pouring spout, but Minty could see the set of her jaw, the clenched teeth, and the stiffen-ing of her back as she reached behind the *settee* and pulled out a little whip. "Do you believe I am stupid, girl?"

"No, ma'am."

"Do you think I cannot see that this room is covered in dirt?"

Minty looked back over the room. Miss Susan was right, the room looked dirtier than when Minty had begun. What went wrong?

"I'll not stand for lazy help." Miss Susan stomped her foot like one of Annie's toddlers. Her voice was becoming more shrill. "Speak up, girl. What have you to say for yourself?"

Minty didn't know what to say. She did know from the rise in Miss Susan's voice and the quiver of her body that nothing she said would help. When white folks got themselves worked up like this, nothing she could say would head off the whipping. Sometimes it just added to the trouble.

"So you choose to stand there insolently defying me?" She stretched out the word *insolently*, seeming to enjoy the sound of the word on her tongue.

Minty moved in preparation for the blow. She had seen enough angry whippings in her life. She turned a quarter turn and brought her elbow up over her ear. The upturned arm kept the whip from slicing across the face, possibly damaging an eye or ear.

If a mistress cut a slave's face too badly, she often later regretted her anger. It became difficult to look at the damage day after day. When friends came to call, it didn't speak well for her character, since a refined woman was expected to exercise self-control. Many a slave was turned out to the field or sold South because of an embarrassing scar.

Annie always said that a whip in the hands of a mistress was worse than one used by a cruel overseer. The overseer took great pleasure in the show of the whipping. He'd tie a slave to a tree or the whipping post and lay thirty-nine lashes across the back. It often flayed the flesh right off the bone, but it rarely maimed him. An angry woman just started flailing and the whip would slice into anything it happened to hit.

"Are you going to answer me, girl?" Miss Susan cracked the whip, catching Minty across the soft underside of her arm, the ends whipping across her neck.

Minty screamed. The first blow was always the worst. It felt like her flesh was on fire. Her scream seemed to make Miss Susan angrier and she began to slash the whip repeatedly. Minty tried dodging the whip. She knew if she ran, she'd escape further blows. The Brodas slaves who lived in the Quarter always said that ladies almost never chased after a slave, whip in hand. If any friends happened to be passing it did not seem ladylike. Running never worked with Mrs. Cook. She didn't care what anyone thought.

Miss Susan was stronger than she looked. Minty lost count of how many times the whip came down. Her screams turned to moans—it took too much energy to scream. As another blow sliced open her neck once more, she screamed again.

"Susan!" It was a woman with a baby. "Whatever are you doing to that poor girl?"

"I told her to dust and sweep this room and she stubbornly refused." Miss Susan dropped the whip and kicked it back behind the *settee*.

"How old are you, child?"

"About eight or nine, ma'am."

"Emily, you need to stay out of household affairs." Miss Susan's eyes flashed at her sister. "It is my job to see that my household help is kept in line."

"Why do you whip the child for failing what she has never

been taught to do?" Miss Emily handed the baby to Miss Susan. "Leave the girl to me for a few minutes and you will see that she will soon learn how to sweep and dust a room."

Miss Susan turned with an angry swish of skirts and left the room. The pile of dust Minty had gathered by the doorway was caught by the hem of her gown and left a trail down the hallway.

"Go to the dustbin on the back entrance and get the dustpan—the scoop with a handle." She looked at Minty. "Wait. First stop at the basin outside the back entrance. There will be a clean rag beside it. Wipe the blood off your cuts. The cooling water should help some."

Minty did as she was told and hurried back. Her neck and her arm were on fire.

"Now, I've dampened the broom ever so slightly. It will keep the dust from flying into the air. Sweep the rug and the floor first, so you'll give the dust time to settle before dusting the furniture."

Minty swept the rug and then the wood floor. The dampness of the broom caused the dust to clump instead of fly.

"Now, sweep the pile into the dustpan and go out and dump it in the dustbin. Put the pan back where you found it."

Minty did it and returned.

"Now, see the air?"

"Yes, ma'am."

"The dust has settled so it's time to dust the furniture."

After Minty dusted and put away the feather duster, Miss Emily looked around the room. "There. Let that headstrong sister of mine find anything wrong with this room." She put her hand on Minty's good shoulder. "Have you ever cared for a baby?"

"Yes, ma'am."

"Lucinda is the fussiest baby I've ever seen. You will have your hands full, child." She paused for a moment. "Do your best to stay out of my sister's way. As beautiful as Susan is, she is angry and unhappy. We all feel the lash of her temper."

Minty looked up to see Miss Susan standing just inside the library door.

## 8
# Oh, Freedom!

Minty was sorry to see Miss Emily leave. In the first weeks of Minty's hire, Miss Emily taught her many household tasks, although caring for the baby took up most of Minty's time.

Miss Emily hadn't exaggerated when she called Baby Lucinda fussy. The baby cried much of each night. At first Minty slept too soundly to hear the baby, but each time Miss Susan was awakened by the baby, she reached for the little whip she kept on a shelf by the bed and slashed it across Minty's neck.

"Wake up, girl." Miss Susan's voice whined at night. It was as if she couldn't be bothered to keep the sweet musical quality of her daytime voice. "I need my sleep to run a household this size and entertain guests for my husband. You must keep that child quiet."

Minty soon learned to sleep lightly. She woke at the first sounds of stirring in the cradle to push on the rocker. The movement usually soothed the baby. Not always.

"Keep that child quiet!" Miss Susan never used Lucinda's name. She was always "that child."

"Yes, ma'am." Minty sat on the floor with the baby on her lap. When Miss Lucinda had a restless night, nothing would help other than holding her. Annie would have called her spoiled. Lately the baby screamed if Minty didn't walk her. Minty was getting more and more tired each day.

Sometimes during the day, Miss Lucinda would sleep in her pram, but mostly she wanted to be held all the time. Minty was glad that she was strong and could walk the baby for hours.

The days and nights seemed to all run together. Sometimes Minty dozed as she held the baby. Once she dreamed she held Nicey in her arms, but instead of those pudgy hands that would pet Minty's cheeks, Minty woke to flailing arms and a screaming baby.

Several times each day, Minty carried the baby outside to the kitchen where Sadie would prepare a bottle.

"Not natural, that's what I say," Sadie would mutter.

"What's not natural?"

"That woman. Having me fixing bottles of cow milk for that *colicky* baby." Sadie had a way of talking half to herself as she moved around the kitchen. "If she don't want to feed her own baby, 'least she could get a wet nurse to do it."

"What's *colicky*, Sadie?" Minty took the warm bottle and gave it to the baby.

"Baby's stomach is sour all the time. Jes' can't get that milk to go down right." Sadie turned the dough out of the bowl onto the floured table. Her brown fists punched the risen dough down. "Jes' not natural." She began kneading the dough. "If that woman would just think about anyone 'sides herself..."

"Is there anything I can do to help Miss Lucinda?"

"Not with her colic, but jigglin' her around don't help her none. She needs to be patted until the gas bubble comes up and then left alone to settle down."

"But I must not allow her to disturb Miss Susan during the day, and when she cries at night, I get whipped."

"Jes' not natural, that's what I say." Sadie turned the kneaded dough back into the bowl to rise again. "Let me see your neck, Minty."

"It's healin' except for this one I got last night."

"Are you usin' that grease I gave you?"

"Yes."

"Still no help for it." Sadie fingered the welts on Minty's neck. "You'll carry scars for the rest of your life."

"Do they look bad?" Minty lifted the baby up to pat her back, bringing up a loud belch. "There you go, Miss Lucinda."

"One good thing 'bout those scars is they'll keep you from the slave block."

"The slave block?"

"When slave traders and buyers see those scars they think 'pure trouble'—a stubborn slave." Sadie chuckled. "Won't nobody want to buy you."

"Then I'll wear my scars proudly if they help me stay near my family." Minty didn't mind being thought stubborn. No one knew how frightened she was most of the time. She handed the bottle back to Sadie. "Thank you for tellin' me 'bout Miss Lucinda's colic. I'll try not to jiggle her so much."

After that, Minty did a little better with the baby when Miss Susan wasn't around. As Miss Lucinda grew, she loved to hear Minty's deep voice. When she told the baby a story, it seemed to quiet her, and when Minty broke into song the baby liked it even better.

"Ch, ch, ch," Minty began.

"Ch, ch, ch," the baby mimicked.

"Ch, ch, ch, ch." Minty speeded up. "Ch, ch, ch, ch." It was the sound of a train gaining speed. Miss Lucinda was fascinated by the sound.

"Train's a comin', woo-o, woo."

The baby clapped her hands as Minty began to sing in her deep voice:

> Git on board, little chillen,
> Git on board, little chillen,
> Git on board, little chillen,
> There's room for many a-more.

Minty leaned her face close to the baby and sang in a quieter voice:

> The gospel train is a-comin',
> I hear it jus' at hand.
> I hear the car wheels movin',
> And rumblin' through the land.

When Minty burst out with the "git on board" part again, the baby laughed out loud.

Git on board, little chillen,
Git on board, little chillen,
Git on board, little chillen,
There's room for many a-more.

Quiet and secretive-like again, Minty sang:

The fare is cheap an' all can go,
The rich an' poor are there.
No second class aboard this train,
No difference in the fare.

When she finished the chorus one last time, Minty drew Miss Lucinda into her lap. In a quiet, soothing voice, Minty began to string words together in her deep voice. She knew if she kept her words smooth, Miss Lucinda would fall asleep in time for Minty to finish some chores.

"That gospel train runs on a secret track, Miss Lucinda. Not on a trestle. Not over the mountain. Not across open fields." Minty took the baby's hands and made motions of trestles, mountains, and fields as she talked. The baby leaned into Minty as she became sleepy. "The gospel train don't go clackety-clack over iron tracks or chug-a, chug-a up steep hills. Do you know where that ol' gospel train goes, Miss Lucinda?"

She could tell by the way the baby's body slumped that Miss Lucinda slept at last. "It's a secret, baby, but that train disappears right into a hole in the ground where a body can't find it. Nobody but Jesus knows where that train goes."

She lifted the sleeping child into her crib. *Why didn't I ask*

*Annie more questions about this Underground Railroad? I just
know it's more than make-believe stories. But what?*

"Araminta." It was Miss Susan calling.

"Coming." Minty lifted her quilt off the trunk and
opened the lid to take out a freshly starched apron. Didn't do
to risk Miss Susan's temper with a soiled apron. As Minty
carefully put her quilt back on the lid, she ran her hand over
the patchwork. It always made her think of home.

"Come here, girl. Let me look at you." Miss Susan tilted
her head to the side as she looked hard at Minty. "Where's
Miss Lucinda?"

"I just got her down for nap, ma'am."

"Run and tell Sadie to ask if Liddie's girl will sit with her.
I need you to wait table for tea."

"Yes, ma'am."

As Minty ran to tell Sadie, she felt that familiar stab of
fear. Whenever Miss Susan was near, Minty never did anything right. As she thought about waiting table, the room
seemed to get smaller and Minty felt her chest tighten. *Why
can't I just go outside? I hate being indoors all day long under the
quick-tempered eye of Miss Susan.*

Minty gave Sadie Miss Susan's message. The old cook
just shook her head and clucked her tongue, but Minty understood. She didn't know the first thing about serving white
folk. *If only I knew where to catch that train. . . .*

"Araminta!" Impatience colored Miss Susan's voice.

"Coming, ma'am."

"Now, I want you to bring the plates of scones and clotted
cream first, y'heah? Are your hands clean, girl?" She grabbed
one of Minty's hands, flipping it from palm to back. She

seemed disappointed to find it clean. "I hope you've not been wasting my soap."

"No, ma'am."

"Where was I before you interrupted? Oh, yes, the scones. Bring them from the kitchen and put them over there." She pointed to a place on the table. "No, wait. Hold the plate by the right side of each of my guests. Or is it the left side?"

Minty was getting confused. How could she hold the plate if she also had a dish of clotted cream? She knew if she asked it would only make her mistress angry. Perhaps she would have time to ask Sadie.

"After you've passed the scones, hold the dish of cream for each guest. Make sure you serve the master first as he is particularly fond of clotted cream." She paused. "No, better not serve him first. Serve the ladies first, but make sure they don't take too much."

Serve him first. Don't serve him first. Put the scones on the table. Don't put the scones on the table. Minty knew trouble was brewing. Miss Susan fluttered about the table, giving orders and changing orders. She didn't know what she wanted, but Minty knew who would be blamed for any mistakes. Whenever Miss Susan was nervous, Minty could do nothing right.

The guests began to arrive. Minty stood by the dining room door. She caught the scent as each lady swept into the parlor. Lilac water, orris root, the spicy smell of lavender, the delicate scent of rose water, and finally, the masculine smells of leather, cigar smoke, and sandalwood joined Miss Susan's jasmine.

Miss Susan visited with her guests. Her voice sounded

musical as she talked and laughed. *So different from her day-to-day voice.* Minty knew anger simmered under the surface.

*Please, God, let me do it right.* Of course, it didn't really matter how well she served—she'd get whipped before the day was over. Whenever Miss Susan got all worked up like today, she lashed out. Minty sometimes wondered if Miss Susan's whippings were a way of easing the anger building up inside herself.

The guests finally made their way into the dining room. The French doors were both opened so the ladies didn't have to squeeze their huge hoop skirts through the doorway. The men pulled chairs out for the ladies and waited patiently while hoops were arranged. If a lady sat too quickly, her hoop might swing up in front like a bell, allowing petticoats to show. To make room for hoops, dress, and petticoats, each lady could only perch on the edge of her chair.

*No wonder the Missus and her friends don't do any work. It is hard enough for them just to move. Maybe they figure they have work enough arranging their silk dresses and keeping their shawls from slipping down their shoulders.* Minty couldn't help thinking about the women in the Quarter. Old Rit and the other women moved with a rhythmic swing to their hips. It was a natural grace.

Minty brought the plate of scones in from the kitchen. Talk and laughter around the table held everyone's attention. Minty slipped in beside each guest. Without even looking at their server, each one took a scone from her plate. Miss Susan took hers last. Though she laughed and talked with the rest of the guests, Miss Susan's eyes never left Minty.

Minty put the plate of scones on the sideboard and

returned to the kitchen for the clotted cream. She paid close attention to balance since the footed bowl only had four tiny crystal feet resting on a slippery crystal plate. The slightest tip would send the bowl crashing to the floor, or worse yet, onto the silken lap of one of the ladies. For the second time that day, she successfully made it around the table.

She brought in the bowl of crushed strawberries and placed it on the table near Miss Susan, just as Sadie said. Next the teapot. Sadie had her pick it up in her right hand and use a fancy napkin to hold the lid.

As she slid in next to the lilac-scented lady in yellow, Miss Susan asked, "Eugenia, do you care for tea?"

When the guest answered that she did, Minty carefully poured the tea. The routine was repeated with each guest. When the empty teapot was taken to the kitchen, the thudding of Minty's heart eased a little. She took the cream pitcher and sugar bowl into the dining room and again went around the table, pouring cream or using the tiny tongs to drop sugar cubes into teacups.

"Araminta, you may retire to the kitchen," Miss Susan finally said. "I will call you if we have need of your services."

"Sadie," Minty said as she sat down near the sink where the cook was working, "I did it without spilling a drop." She felt fluttery and worn out all at the same time.

"You done fine." Sadie seemed troubled.

"Is something wrong?"

"Not 'bout the way you waited table. You done jes' fine, chile." Sadie took her time. "Jes' watch out, Minty." She lowered her voice. "That woman's wound tighter'n a pocket watch."

"What do you mean?"

"I seen her like this b'fore. She gets herself all worked up 'bout company . . . like, do they talk 'bout her, or flirt with Master, or maybe they don't pay 'nough attention to her. Don't matter what. When they leave, jes' watch out." Sadie let a big breath out through her lips. "That's all I got to say 'bout that."

When Miss Susan walked out onto the veranda to say good-bye to the last guests, Minty went into the dining room to begin clearing up. What a mess was left. Napkins lay in the crushed strawberries, and cream was left on the plates. Tea was sloshed onto saucers. Scones were half eaten and broken into bits. To someone who never quite had enough to eat, Minty felt shame for Miss Susan and her guests, looking at the waste.

Even the sugar bowl had been knocked over. The tongs lay on the cloth beside a sugar cube. Minty had never tasted real sugar, but she knew it tasted like the cane Old Rit once let them chew. How Minty loved the sweet taste of cane. As she righted the sugar bowl, she took the spilled cube and dropped it into her pocket.

"Well, I never!" Miss Susan had been standing inside the doorway. "I positively will not stand for a common thief in my household, Araminta Ross." Her voice had risen in pitch and volume until everyone in the house could hear the accusation. "I saw you steal that cube of sugar. Even my husband saw you!"

"Now, Susan." Master used the same soothing voice he used with his horses. "Don't you be taking out your temper on—"

"You stay out of it!" She was stamping her foot like a child. "I will manage *my* property any way I see fit."

*Her property? Her property!* Minty clamped her mouth shut, letting the air come out her nostrils. She was sick of doing it Old Rit's way. *I hate slavery and I hate Miss Susan. I worked so hard to please her and . . .* Minty began backing out of the dining room as Miss Susan continued to scream. Once out of the room, she turned and ran, pumping her legs as hard as she could, out the back door and down toward the creek.

With Master's friends still close at hand, Minty knew Miss Susan would not come running after a slave. Besides, she could hear Miss Susan and the master arguing.

As her feet beat a rhythm on the thick grass she began to hum a tune deep in her throat:

> Oh, freedom. Oh, freedom. Oh, freedom, over me.
> And before I be a slave, I'll be buried in my grave,
> And go home to my Lord and be free.

*Oh, if I could just find that freedom train,* Minty thought as she ran farther and farther away from Miss Susan's screams.

# Steal Away

"Wade in the water, child."

Minty looked around to see who spoke. Nobody was there. Who said the words then? *They must be runnin' through my head from the song*, Minty thought as she ran beside the creek trying to get far away from Miss Susan's whip.

"Wade in the water."

This time Minty realized the words were not spoken. They just whispered in her head and sort of came out her lips. Could it be the voice of God? Angels? The devil himself? She quickly dismissed the devil. The words were whispered with love and it was the same voice she had known her whole life. Though Minty wasn't sure she'd ever heard the voice aloud, it often sort of hummed underneath her fear and loneliness. She heard it in her dreams. Yes, she knew that voice.

"Here I am, Lord," Minty said. She felt funny saying that, but she remembered hearing her father tell how God came to Moses in the burning bush. That was Moses' answer to God.

"Here I am." She reached down and untied her shoes and slipped them off her feet, just like Moses did. She took off her apron and laid it alongside the shoes. Her chest hurt from running. *There's no way I can outrun them. I don't know what else to do.*

She slipped down the creek bank and began to wade up the stream. It wasn't deep like the river where Mr. Cook ran his trapline. It only came up to her waist. The stones under Minty's feet were smooth from being tumbled by the stream. She waded close to the high bank cut away by last winter's torrents, under a kind of overhang formed by roots and grassy turf. Spotting her from the direction of Miss Susan's would be impossible without leaning way over the bank.

She hadn't waded far when she came to a crevice caused by a tangle of roots and deadfall. Her knees were still wobbly and her chest tight from fear. Wedging herself into the crevice, she rested. Before long she felt her body getting lighter, as if she could fly.

"Master, look!"

Minty woke with a start. She had been flying like a bird above the Brodas Plantation in her dream, but she woke to find her body still firmly wedged into the crevice. At the sound of excited voices on the bank downstream, she froze.

"It's the girl's shoes and apron, alright." This was the voice of the master.

There was a long silence followed by the master's voice again. "I'll be jiggered. Whatever was the girl thinking? Nigras can't swim and this water is swift. How do I tell Brodas that my wife's uncontrollable temper sent his slave off to drown herself? Lord, have mercy."

"Want me to take up these shoes and things, suh?"

"Of course. They can be used again." Master sounded impatient. "Look around a little upstream, just in case, while I have someone back at the house fetch the patrollers to bring their dogs. They need to look downstream for the body."

"Yes, suh."

"Don't stay out here too long because you don't have a pass."

"Yes, suh."

The buzz of mosquitoes was the only sound Minty heard. She strained her ears but couldn't catch any movement at all. After what seemed like a long time she heard a deep voice softly singing from the place she'd last heard the master:

> Steal away, steal away,
> Steal away to Jesus.
> Steal away, steal away home.
> I ain't got long to stay here.

The voice got even quieter. Minty strained to hear.

> Steal away, steal away,
> Steal away upstream.

Minty listened close. That wasn't how the words went.

> Steal away, steal away now,
> I ain't e'en fixin' to look here.

And one more verse:

Steal away, steal away,
Steal away to freedom.
Steal away, in the creek,
Dogs can't even follow.

Minty understood that the slave was giving her a message. She slipped out of the crevice and continued upstream, keeping close to the bank. *Thank you, friend.*

It was hard work wading against the current. *How'd I know to head upstream? It was that voice. The patroller's bloodhounds can't follow scent in water—but I if I hadn't obeyed the Lord to wade in the water, I'd have left an easy trail to follow.*

Minty continued moving through the stream. Her legs ached from pushing against the current. Her ankles felt so cold that her teeth began to clatter. She just kept moving through the stream, knowing each step took her farther away from Master and Miss Susan.

To keep her mind off the cold, she began to sing a song in her mind. *Oh, freedom, oh, freedom.* The words kept repeating in her mind as she pushed forward.

Minty's plight hit her all at once. *Why am I singing about freedom?* She didn't even know how to get to freedom. She was Araminta Ross, Old Rit and Ben's little girl, and she was a fugitive slave. If the patrollers found her they'd whip her and return her. Master would also whip her. Fugitives were often sold South.

*A fugitive.* She continued to wade upstream but no further songs marked her way.

She'd been wading upstream for what seemed like hours. She came to several forks where she could have taken another downstream fork and headed off in a different direction, but she kept remembering the slave's advice to head upstream. A bridge crossing the stream gave her a place to hide out of the water in order to rest. Pilings had been driven deep into the streambed. Cross timbers gave her a dry place to hide. She poked around with a stick to make sure she'd not be sharing her hidey-hole with too many spiders. Just the thought made her shiver.

As soon as she wedged herself in, she began to feel sleepy.

Rackety, rackety, rackety! The noise of a wagon crossing from the far side of the bridge woke her. She pulled herself into an even tighter ball. Could anyone see her?

"Pull up, Saul. Ain't Master gonna know if we stop off for a smoke. Jes' get over the bridge and pull up by that tree." The voice came from almost over Minty's head as the wagon rackety-racked over the wooden bridge.

"Reckon it won't hurt none. Whoa, whoa, boys."

The wagon had crossed the bridge, but Minty could hear the men talking plain as day.

"No one ever gonna find out. Good thing the missus is so fussy 'bout smells. T'Master Stebbins builds the pigsty near a mile from the Big House." The man laughed and continued, "He doesn't think that it takes us near an hour to bring slops out ever' evenin' after supper."

The old man called Saul laughed along with him. "I call it dee-vine providence, that's what I call it. Ain't no overseer gonna trouble hisself to come out this far. You one lucky man, Rufus."

"Haulin' water outta the creek at first light and muckin' the pen takes me a good hour or two. I get back with only one hour, mebbe two in the field till the bell rings for dinner. I have to work with the hands in the field till supper, but when all the slops and leftovers been collected, I take off in the wagon and head back out here."

"That so?"

"Summerime I get here long 'bout twilight, slops the hogs quick-like, and I can ride by the ol' Cole place to see my kids and my woman, if I hurry."

Minty heard the wagon rattle off. They must have finished their tobacco. She needed to remember the direction so she could find that pigsty.

She remembered the story Ben told called "The Prodigal Son." Jesus first told it a long time ago—it was in the Bible. Her father could spin that story till you could hardly breathe for waiting.

The part she remembered now was when the runaway son lived with the pigs and ate right alongside them. Her stomach growled so loudly she'd been afraid the slaves would hear. They said they were taking slops to the pigs—the leftovers from supper. Perhaps she could get enough to hold her over until she figured out where to go. With the pigsty so far from the rest of their plantation it could be the safest hiding place of all.

Minty waited under the bridge until the wagon carrying the two slaves came back over the bridge. When it was safe to climb out, she quickly found the wagon tracks. They were easy enough to follow even though night had fallen. She heard grunting long before she could see the pigsty.

She hurried toward the noise, hoping they hadn't slopped in all the leftovers yet. In one pen lay a big sow with a whole row of newborn piglets. The sow looked too tired to get up to eat.

Minty slipped through the rails and started to move toward the feeding trough. She never considered it dangerous, but the huge sow shot to her feet, spilling baby pigs as she charged. The grunting of the sow and squealing of piglets ripped through the quiet evening. Minty managed to scramble back through the fence just ahead of the angry pig. She let out her breath in a whoosh. Did the men hear the noise? Minty sat motionless as the minutes ticked by.

The angry sow continued to weave back and forth across the pen. Sorry for disturbing them, Minty watched as the sow just missed stepping on her babies several times. *I wonder if Jesus' Prodigal Son had this problem?*

She came around the far side of the pen and slipped into the tight space where two pens joined. *I hope there are no spiders here.* But she was so hungry she didn't even poke around to see. By sitting on the ground and reaching into the sow's pen all the way up to the shoulder, her arm could stretch into the trough. She couldn't see a thing since, in order to get in far enough, her head was turned away and her cheek pressed against the rail. She'd have to feel her way to any edible scraps.

Deep in the trough was just wet stuff. The thought of it caused her stomach to lurch, but she was so hungry that she ached. She had to stop acting like a baby.

The dry slops seemed to be toward the sides. *There. That feels like sweet corn.* She brought out a partly eaten cob. It looked perfectly good except for two or three rows around the cob. *Must have belonged to someone with only a few teeth left who was too tired after a day in the field to work at eating corn.* She put the cob in her lap and stretched her hand back into the trough. The sow had settled down with her babies again. This time Minty hit a pan-shaped hunk of what must be corn *pone*. She pulled it out and looked it over. The bottom was blackened. Minty laughed out loud. "Thank You, Jesus." She pictured the cook in the Big House. She must have been distracted and allowed the cornbread to burn. Rather than cut the bottom off and risk a whipping, she hid a perfectly good *pone* in the slops bucket.

Minty slid out of the crawl space between the pens and sat out on the grass under a tree to eat. She wiped the food off as best she could, but she didn't let herself think about where she got it. *I'll just think about it as manna—the food God gave to Moses in the wilderness. Just like the children of Israel, I won't worry about tomorrow's food either.*

With the sound of the hoot owls and whippoorwills hollering at each other, Minty crawled back into the crawl space to sleep. This time she took a willow *switch* and checked carefully for spiders.

Luckily, at Miss Susan's, she had learned to sleep lightly enough to wake the instant Miss Lucinda cried. She needed to sleep just as lightly now. She prepared herself to wake the moment she heard wagon wheels on the wooden bridge.

Before falling asleep, she remembered her precious quilt lying atop the trunk in Miss Susan's room. The soft grunts of the sleeping pigs mingled with the muffled sobs of the lonely girl until a gentleness sort of hummed her to sleep.

Minty woke to the sound of far-off wagon wheels. She scrambled out of her hiding place into the nearby woods. She needed to stay close enough to hear when Rufus finished watering the pigs and mucking out the pens. She knew it was safer to keep herself tucked in between the pens than be out in the open where her scent might carry to any bloodhounds searching for her. Of course she smelled more like a pig than anything else right now.

As she moved into the woods, she thought back to when she was recovering from measles. *What had Annie said about the Underground Railroad? She didn't think it was a real train or even a road underground. That's right. She said she figured it was the folks from Up North who were trying to help slaves get to freedom.*

*I need to get to freedom.* But Minty didn't know how to find the people who helped. She didn't even know which way was Up North. *Why didn't I ask Ben more questions?* Her father could tell exactly where a body was headed by looking at the stars. He'd feel around on the trunks of the trees to see which side had moss growing on it. Did the north side grow moss? Or was it the west side? The east side?

*How can I get to freedom when I don't know where it is?* Minty knew that instead of worrying about whether she'd have courage when the time came, she should have prepared herself. Moses didn't go to Pharaoh until he was ready to lead his people to freedom.

As each day passed, Minty got hungrier and hungrier. Most times the slops were too wet to fish out. She kept remembering the words of Annie, "Once a body be free, ain't never goin' come back to slavery, child. Ain't never." *But what if you couldn't make your way to freedom?*

Courage. She always worried if she'd have enough courage to run. When she took off running out the door of Miss Susan's, she didn't even have time to decide. Her feet made the decision long before her head agreed.

Now she wondered if she had enough courage to go back. This time she had plenty of time to think about it. She knew if she ever wanted to make a run for freedom, she needed to be prepared. "Lord Jesus," she prayed, "give me courage to go back and face my enemy. And then give me the chance to prepare, like Moses did, to move toward freedom."

Her legs were wobbly and her head was muzzy, but she retraced her steps back to the bridge. As she slid into the water, the cold shocked her. *Good, that will keep me going for a time.* When she had chosen to go upstream, she never thought that, weak and hungry several days later, she'd be glad to have the current downstream to help her make her way back.

※　　　※　　　※　　　※

"Miss Susan, Miss Susan!" Minty woke to the sound of Sadie's voice. "Araminta done come back on her own." Sadie emphasized *on her own*. "Willie found her laid out at the same place on the bank where Master found her shoes last week."

"Ugh. She's nothing but skin stretched over bone. Get some of that corn mush down the stupid girl's throat, Sadie." It was Miss Susan. "Bill, go tell Master to get the wagon hitched. Good thing he didn't pay the patrollers any money to find this one."

Minty could feel Sadie lift her shoulders and spoon the mush into her mouth. The half-starved girl wasn't so far gone that she didn't notice that it felt warm and tasted wonderful. *Mmm.* She was so tired and hungry that it hardly mattered what Miss Susan would do.

Next time Minty woke, Willie was putting her into the back of a wagon. Was she being sold South?

Miss Susan came out of the house with a bundle in her arms. "Take this quilt. I don't want to have to dispose of it." She pulled her shawl around her and climbed up beside Willie.

"Ghee-up." Willie clucked to the horse to get them moving.

The clip-clop, clip-clop of the horses made it hard for Minty to think. She knew she should be alert, but . . .

Thump! Minty could hear the sound of her body hitting wood as Willie dropped her.

"I said, drop her and get back to the wagon, boy." It was Miss Susan. In a different voice she asked, "Is Mr. Brodas at home?"

*Mr. Brodas? Can it be? Rather than get whipped, burned, or sold South, I'm to come home? I must be dreamin'.*

"Certainly, I'm at home." It was Master. "Who wishes to see me without an invitation, Cicero?" Master came out onto the veranda, his hand over his eyes to shield them from the glare of the late-afternoon sun.

"It is I, Mr. Brodas."

"Miss Susan, forgive me. I was not expecting you. Is your husband with you?" He looked over at Willie, now sitting in the wagon, before turning to Miss Susan again. "Do come in."

Just then he saw Araminta, who had pulled herself up to a sitting position, still clutching her quilt. He now understood why Miss Susan had come.

"No," she said, "I'm here to return this stubborn slave my husband hired from you. She wasn't worth a *sixpence* to begin with, but after running off, she's not worth the food to fill her back up." Minty could see the temper tantrum that brewed beneath the surface. Instead of letting the anger loose, the young woman turned around and stomped off the veranda in a huff. "You decide what to do with her. I wash my hands."

"Someone get Old Rit and tell her the girl is back again." Brodas shrugged his shoulders and turned to go back into the house. "Good thing the woman didn't ask me to return the hire fee." He smiled. "Someone get her off my veranda before the missus catches a whiff."

## 10
## Keep
## A-Inchin' Along

The years passed and, except for a few times he briefly hired her out, Master Brodas allowed Minty to remain. Annie said he told Cicero that he felt sorry Minty had been so badly used. The wounds inflicted by Miss Susan's whip eventually all healed, but they left thickly raised scars crisscrossing the skin on her neck and shoulders.

No one ever tried to give Minty an indoor job again, which suited her just fine. Even her mother could see that Minty was happiest when working outdoors. Old Rit just thanked the Lord that her Araminta could grow up close at hand. When they issued her a long homespun skirt from the storehouse that fall, she knew she was leaving childhood behind.

One day, Old Rit called Minty over before she left for the field. "Honey-girl, I look at you and I jes' see my mother, plain as day. Why, you are 'most a woman fully growed."

Minty savored her mother's words.

"This here's a head cloth." Old Rit took out a strip of freshly woven red cloth. "Women wrap this round 'n' round they heads to keep the sun off. When it beats down hard 'n' hot, you jes' dip it in the wash bucket and tie it soppin' wet onto your head. It he'ps keeps you cooler."

Old Rit showed her how to wrap and tie it. "Mos'ly, we jes' wear it 'cause it makes us beau'ful." After having her look at the wrap in the scrap of mirror, her mother said, "I picked turkey red for you 'cause your skin is smooth and black as ebony. 'Nothing will look half as pretty on my Harriet,' I thought."

Harriet? Minty couldn't believe her ears. Was she finally to get her grown-up name?

Old Rit began to call Minty Harriet. At first nearly everyone still called her Minty, but as they got used to it, they slowly changed over. First with a "Mint—um . . . Harriet' and finally with a clear "Harriet."

At thirteen years old, Harriet only stood five feet tall, but it was said that she was as strong as any man on the plantation. After working indoors at both the Cooks' and Miss Susan's, there was nothing she liked better than working in the field all day long. When the bell rang for dinner, she stretched achy muscles and lifted her face to the sky, opening her mouth to let the sunshine deep inside.

"Harriet." It was a workday like any other when the overseer singled her out. "Harriet Ross."

Harriet looked up from the row of corn. "Yes, suh?"

"Master wants you to meet him down at the landing by the river."

"Yes, suh."

"And no dawdling on the way, or you'll feel the end of my whip." He snapped the leather tip against his boot. "You run, girl, y'hear?"

"Yes, suh."

*Not again!* Harriet glanced at Rit to see if she'd overheard. Rit's eyebrows drew together in worry, making deep furrows on her forehead. Harriet looked at her mother for a long minute, praying this didn't mean another good-bye. As she hurried off to meet the master, she heard the sandpapery sound of her mother's fidgety fingers.

"Here she is, gentlemen." Master Brodas held out his arm toward Harriet.

What was this about? A group of men were standing around him. Was Master holding some sort of spur-of-the-moment slave auction? No. Harriet couldn't see anyone who looked like a speculator or slave trader. She'd often seen one or another of these men riding by the fields on their way up the lane toward the Big House. She figured they were Master's friends.

"Why, you old fox, Brodas, whatever are you up to?" asked one of the men. "She's only a girl." He paused, looking her up and down as if sizing up a feeder pig. "And a runty one at that."

"Just put your money where your mouth is, Cole." He turned to the group. "Time to place your bets, gentlemen." Mr. Brodas took out a small leather-covered book and began to write. One by one the men came up and spoke to him, and he recorded what they told him.

Harriet couldn't figure out what was going on.

"Harriet, I been telling these men how strong you are. Fact is, I told them you could load those *hogsheads* of tobacco onto that barge. After you do that, I want you to lift those barrels of molasses on board. Then, after you hoist those bales of cotton onto the deck, I've told them that you can tow the barge to that fallen tree."

So that was it. Master had a bet with these men.

"Don't let me down, girl," Master whispered.

Harriet felt that familiar closing-in feeling. Not that she wasn't strong enough. She knew she was strong. Ever since she returned from Miss Susan's she decided to be ready in case she ever had opportunity to set out again. She wanted to be able to walk upstream for hours without growing weary. She might even need to be strong enough to hold off an angry sow or outrun a pack of bloodhounds.

Day after day, she worked in the fields, weeding, hoeing, or picking, until her muscles screamed. Rather than slow down or change pace, as the others did, she pushed on. She learned that by working past the soreness, she grew a little stronger every day.

Once, during the winter, a storm blew a huge tree limb across the road leading to the Quarter. The men just stood around looking and talking. Harriet welcomed a chance to test her newfound strength, but even more, she thought it great fun to show up the young men. Harriet squatted down, wrapped her arms around the limb, and, keeping her back straight, used the strength of her legs to lift the heavy branch. Those watching laughed and teased as the branch moved little by little. When she finished, she looked up to see the overseer watching as well. He had been called to bring a horse so that the men could tow it off the road. Harriet knew it never did any good to come under the overseer's eye.

No, she wasn't afraid she couldn't win the bet for Master. She was strong and if it could be done, she'd do her best to do it. What she hated was being treated like a beast of burden—a workhorse to wager on. What was wrong with these men? Didn't they see that she was a child of God like them? What should she do, obey her master or stand against the evil?

She stood still for a full minute before she leaned over to roll the first *hogshead* of tobacco down toward the barge. As it rolled down the last incline, she ran in front of it, squatted down toward the bale, and hoisted the bundle onto her shoulder. She used her strong legs to stand under the weight and managed to get it onto the barge. She rolled it to the far corner and repeated the process.

The whole time she was working, the men hooted and called, making jokes and trying to disturb her concentration. Minty tried to ignore them. As she lifted a barrel of molasses, she remembered hearing the story of the people who lined the road to mock Jesus as He carried His cross. *Father, let me carry my burdens cheerfully. Make me fit for the journey ahead.*

As she lifted the last bale of cotton aboard the barge, the men became quiet. Harriet thought about the journey ahead as she continued her prayer. *Make me strong for the task You've set before me.* She didn't mean this silly wager. She wanted to be ready to seek freedom when the time came. Maybe God would use her like He used Moses.

She took the thick rope in her hands as she stood on the bank. She pulled but the barge didn't move. Was it caught on something? Normally the barge would have had a pole man to hold it away from the bank, but she'd have to try to pull toward her and away from the bank all at once.

The barge rode low on the water. Maybe it was too heavy for her to pull. As she dug her legs into the grass and tensed her body to pull, a deep song welled up:

Keep a-inchin' along, keep a-inchin' along.
Massa Jesus is comin' by 'n' by.

As she paused at each break, she let out a rush of air, like a loud "huh," and pulled with all her strength. Inch by inch the barge began to move down the river. When she finally reached the fallen tree, the muscles in her legs and shoulders cramped. She let go of the rope and sank to the ground, waiting for the cramps to ease.

The men had followed her, slapping Master on the back. "Congratulations, Brodas," said one. "This is one bet I'm happy to pay."

"I wouldn't have missed this for the world," said another. "You are something else, Old Man."

One by one the men handed money over to Master and he checked them off his book. They all left together, talking and laughing, but since Master didn't tell her to get right back to the field, she lay in the cool grass.

Why was it that she loved teasing the boys in the Quarter with her strength, but hated performing for the entertainment of these men? Refusing Master hadn't seemed worth it. Was it because she lacked courage to refuse? *I remember when Ruby ran. I worried that I didn't have courage to seek freedom, but when the time came to run from Miss Susan's, I never thought of courage. My feet just took me away.*

She looked at the barge. *Now I worry that I don't have*

*courage to stand against evil.* She thought back to Miss Susan's. *Running is sometimes easier than standing.* Like today—it seemed easier to perform for the men than to stand up to them.

The hardest thing she ever did was return to Miss Susan's. So what takes the most courage? To run? To stand? To return? She didn't know. *Lord Jesus, help me be strong for You. Help me to stand when I need to take a stand, to run when You call me to freedom, and to return when You call me back.*

When Harriet returned to the Quarter, everyone was talking about the bet. Master sent word that he wished to see her later, along with her father. Harriet walked with Ben to the Big House after supper and waited until Master came out onto the veranda.

"Ben, this is some girl you have."

"Yes, suh."

"She's as strong as any man on this plantation."

"Yes, suh."

Changing the subject, he asked, "How you doing on that stand of old growth timber?"

"It's comin' slow, suh, but we's taking time to cut the timber clean and haul it carefully so's not to damage saplings."

"Good, good." Master glanced over at Harriet, then back at Ben. "I called you here because I want to add to your crew."

"Thank you, suh. We can use the help."

"Go to the shed and pick out another ax. This girl of yours is about the best help I can give you."

Harriet could hardly keep her face from breaking into a smile. It wouldn't do to let the master see that she wanted something too badly, but how could she keep from showing her joy?

"That all right with you, girl?" Master looked straight at Harriet.

"Yes, suh." She kept her head down, but deep inside she could hardly keep the joy from bubbling over.

On the way back to the Quarter, they stopped at the toolshed and Ben chose an ax for Harriet. The smooth hardwood handle felt good in her hand. She proudly carried it back to the cabin where Old Rit and Annie waited.

That day marked the beginning of a happy time in Harriet's life. She still had to listen to screams of slaves being whipped for one thing or another, but she no longer worked in the fields. She worked side by side with her father. They woke before dawn and carried their dinner buckets with them as they walked the long timber road to the patch of old-growth wood. They usually marked their journey with song —her father's rumbly bass blending with her own husky tenor. Everyone on the plantation recognized Harriet's voice. The deep voice that followed her bout of measles never left. It gave her a sound like no other. Sometimes, back in the Quarter, people caught the faint murmuring of their singing as she and her father cleared brush long into the night. Harriet loved those nights with her father.

"Ben, how can I use the stars to find my way at night?"

"You need to use the North Star," her father answered.

"How can I tell which one is the North Star?"

He pointed up to the sky. "See that clump of stars that looks like a drinkin' gourd?"

Harriet squinted and finally located the group. "Yes."

"They call 'em the Big Dipper. Now, look for the two bright stars on the far edge of the dipper. Iffen you follow the line with your finger, they point you right to the North Star. See how bright? It sits at the end of the Little Dipper." Ben helped her find them. "Don't it look like the Big Dipper pours into the Little Dipper?"

"If it did, wouldn't the Little Dipper be like the cup that runneth over?"

Ben laughed. "The position of the stars changes with the seasons, but one thing never changes . . . the North Star always points north. Always. Find that ol' North Star and you can count on findin' your way."

Harriet loved working with her father. He knew everything about God's world. Even Master Brodas said her father predicted the weather better than anyone. Ben could tell how big a crop to expect in any given year. By noticing the thickness of an animal's coat he knew whether to expect a hard winter or an easy one. He could even tell how old a tree was by looking at a slice of the trunk. Harriet wanted to learn as much as she could from her father.

"Can I tell which way is north by watching the geese?" She peppered him with questions every time they were alone.

"Tis true the geese fly south in the fall and head back north in the spring, but a goose ain't a dependable sign. I seen 'em circle 'round and 'round lookin' for a place to rest. Sometimes I even watch 'em backtrack for a time. No, not a dependable sign, those geese." Ben looked hard at his daughter. "Why you so interested in north, Harriet?"

"North's where freedom lies." Harriet never hid things from her father.

"You not planning on running, is you, girl?" Ben looked deep into her eyes, almost as if to memorize her.

"No, Ben." She continued working awhile before she said, "Just gettin' ready for when the time comes." She thought of what her mother always said, "By 'n' by."

"Hmm." He was quiet for a time. "You'll let me know, child, before you decide, won't you?"

Harriet just put her arms around him. She had lots more to find out first.

"Harriet, this ol' daddy is proud of you. Not jes' because you work hard. No." He leaned back and looked at her. "Times is good for us jes' now. Mos' our family still be together and you 'n' me work way out here away from all the trouble. I watch you. 'Spite of our good fortune, you ain't never forgettin' how bad it is to take babies away from mamas. You still ain't forgettin' that it's evil for a man to own a man."

"No, Ben, I can't never forget."

"That's why I'm proud of you, Harriet."

That night she burrowed under her quilt, listening for the longest time to the sounds of her family sleeping. Times like these, she didn't know if she ever wanted to leave. Before she fell asleep, she recognized the words of the song that she couldn't get out of her head:

> Go down, Moses,
> Way down in Egypt-land.
> Tell ol' Pharaoh
> To let My people go.

The one line that kept running over and over was: "Oppressed so hard they could not stand."

Harriet burrowed deeper into her quilt, thinking of Ruby who escaped and her sisters who were sold South. Who knew if she'd ever have the courage to stand up to slavery? She remembered the question her mother often repeated, "How long, O Lord?"

As she drifted off to sleep a new song seemed to carry over into her dreams: "God's goin' trouble the waters."

# 11

# It's Me, O Lord

"Time to quit."

The sound of axes stopped. So did the rhythmic humming the timber cutters used to keep pace with one another.

It felt strange to be quitting work when the morning sun was still bright. Harriet and her father made their way back to the Quarter along with the rest of the timber crew. Today was a special day.

As they neared the cabins, a crowd of excited children ran out to meet them. "We goin' to a shuckin', we goin' to a shuckin'," they sang as they danced in circles.

Just then the conch blew, calling the field hands home. Harriet didn't think the children could get any more worked up, but they ran toward the fields to meet the workers, singing and slapping rhythms with their hands.

Propping her ax in her corner of the cabin, Harriet went to wash up in the tub outside. "Old Rit?"

"Um?"

"I'm goin' by Annie's cabin and walk with her to the corn shuckin'." Whenever anyone on the plantation said corn, they drew the sound way out until it sounded like *cawn*.

"Git there soon's you can. I hear they got a heap o' corn to shuck. We want to git it done fast-like so's we have plenty o' time to frolic. Uncle Eben's bringin' his fiddle and says he's fixin' to call figgers to you young 'uns." Old Rit had a lilt in her voice. "Don't dawdle."

Harriet walked quickly over to Annie's. She loved to dance, so her mother didn't have to tell her twice. There was nothing, save Christmas, as much fun as a corn shucking.

"Annie!" Harriet called from the yard. "I came to walk with you to the shuckin'."

"Why, thank ye kindly, Miss Harriet." The old woman made a curtsey of sorts. "Annie'll be much obliged to 'company you, though I figgert a purt' girl like you be fixin' to walk out with one of them good-lookin' bucks."

Harriet laughed. "Oh, Annie. No boy wants to walk out with a scrawny little girl who's stronger than them."

"When time comes to sashay 'round the floor, we jes' see 'bout that." Annie wrapped her shoulders with her best shawl and they set out to the crossroads.

"Old Rit says that the masters have a heap o' corn for us to shuck," Harriet said.

"Nothin' like the old days," said Annie. "I 'members when we git together with six or sebbin other plantations for a shuckin' and they be piles o' corn as high as the Big House."

"That so?" Harriet knew that if she said, "That so?" it would keep Annie telling stories all night long.

"Shor' 'nuff. Now all we got is the Barretts's Plantation and the Brodas's Plantation and two piles of corn."

"But Annie, it's enough for a good contest, isn't it?" Harriet loved the competition. Row after row of corn would be laid out. When the bell sounded, the shuckers began to strip the husks off the ears of corn, each worker trying to get to the end of the row first.

"We'll soon see, child, we'll soon see." Annie made her um-um-um sound as they neared the sound of singing and clapping.

"Somethin' wrong, Annie?" Harriet had long ago learned to read Annie's worry sounds.

"No. Ol' Annie jes' borrowin' trouble." She slowed her step. "I hear tell that they be a heap of trouble over to the Barrett place. That overseer they got is meaner 'n a cornered wildcat. Barrett folks is plum worn out from the whippins and the work."

"That so?"

"I jes' hope they kick up they heels and have some frolic t'night."

The singing led them to the crossroads between the lanes leading to the Brodas place and the Barrett place. The only building was the country store. Any slave who was able to put a few pennies by looked forward to a visit to the store when the work was done.

Harriet knew that the first shucking had begun. She heard one of the work songs:

Watch the sun; see how she run.
Never let her catch you with yer work undone.

Harriet stepped up to be in line for the next shucking round. Not many girls or even women wanted to go against the men, but Harriet never shied away from a contest. As she waited, she watched one of the men from the Barrett place. He waited off to the side and kept looking around.

Before long it was Harriet's turn. She stepped up to one of eight long lines of piled corn. One of the Barrett men, Jube, was making a fuss.

"My line is bigger'n all the others," he said.

His fuss just made everything take longer. At this rate they would never get done in time for the dance.

"Let me take his line," said Harriet. "Then we can get on with it."

The crowd jeered as the girl traded places with Jube. He outweighed her by several *stone* and had at least another foot above her five feet in height.

"A girl ain't in the contest to win, so it don't matter none anyway," he said to the laughing crowd.

"Um, um, um," said Annie with an evil chuckle. "Poor boy."

When the bell sounded, the crowd fell silent. The eight shuckers began to work. It took a few minutes for each to find his rhythm.

Harriet caught hers to the sound of "It's Me, O Lord." She grabbed an ear, pulled the husk off, and threw it in the bushel basket, all in the space of one line.

It's me, it's me, it's me, O Lord,
Standin' in the need of prayer.
It's me, it's me, it's me, O Lord,
Standin' in the need of prayer.

By the time she'd sung the chorus under her breath, she'd shucked four ears. The men had chosen different songs and different rhythms, but the crowd could always pick out Harriet's voice and soon joined her singing.

As she moved along the line, she saw that she was staying apace with the men. *I guess I won't be asked for many dances,* she thought with a laugh. But it was worth it.

> It's me, it's me, it's me, O Lord,
> Standin' in the need of prayer.

The crowd began to pick up the tempo of the song. Harriet had everything to do to keep up, but she wasn't about to be beaten by a row of corn. She saw, from the corner of her eye, that one man had dropped out. She was ahead of four of the men. Another man was even with her. Only the big man who traded piles was ahead of her.

> It's me, it's me, it's me, O Lord,
> Standin' in the need of prayer.

One by one as the work went on, the men dropped out. Most of them said this was too good a contest to miss. Finally it was Harriet and Jube. The crowd was singing faster and faster as they were nearing the ends of their rows. Harriet was working as fast as she could.

"I quit." It was Jube. "I can't even think with all this *caterwaulin'*."

The crowd roared with laughter as Harriet continued to

the end. Annie brought her a dipper of cool water as her father came over to help her to an old crate to catch her breath.

The contests continued until the last cob was thrown in a basket. Everyone agreed that nothing was as exciting as the contest between Harriet and Jube.

Before dark, boards were laid across sawhorses and the food was spread. There were smoked hams and preserves, greens, peas, fried chicken with cracklin' gravy, and all sorts of sweet things. Only Christmas offered a meal such as this one.

As Harriet took her plate and filled it at the table, she saw the nervous Barrett slave again. *Why is he so jumpy? And why doesn't he join in the meal?* All of a sudden she understood. The man was going to make a run for freedom.

She looked around for the Barrett overseer. He was across the clearing, but he was alert. *No. This is not a good time. Don't run.* There was nothing she could do from this far away. She continued to watch as she ate. When she finished she put her plate down as she moved closer to the slave.

She almost reached him when the fidgeting stopped and he took off like a rabbit let out of a trap. Didn't the slave know that in an easygoing crowd a frantic movement would draw immediate attention? The overseer moved almost as fast. Harriet followed along with several others.

The slave ran into the store, probably hoping to hide, but the overseer followed him in there. Harriet followed and stood inside the door. The man was cornered.

Getting out his whip, the overseer yelled to Harriet, "Hold him so I can tie him up. I'm goin' to whip the clothes right off his back!" He was livid.

Harriet couldn't move a muscle.

"Girl." The overseer was so angry that he spat the words out. "You there. I said hold him."

*Courage to stand.* Harriet almost heard the words.

*Where did that come from?* Harriet remembered when she prayed for courage when the time came. Courage to run, courage to stand, and courage to return, if need be. Somehow she knew she was being called to stand. "Here I am, Lord."

"Don't mumble, girl. Just get in and hold him or I'll flay the very hide off you." The overseer was fumbling with ropes and his bullwhip.

The young man saw his chance and bolted for the door.

"Stop him! Stop him, I say!"

After he ran out the door, Harriet took two firm steps sideways, blocking the low door completely. *Run. Run and be free.*

The overseer, in a fit of rage, grabbed one of the heaviest weights off the grocer's scale and flung it at Harriet with every ounce of strength he possessed.

She heard an explosion—a kind of cracking explosion that caused her to fall to the floor. Her arm ended up under her head somehow and she could feel something warm and sticky running over her arm and onto the floor. From a long way off, she heard Ben saying over and over, "Lord have mercy, Lord have mercy."

She gently lifted off the floor. Her body no longer felt heavy as it floated above the room until Harriet was flying. With arms outstretched she looked down to see rivers and fields and . . .

## 12
# Let My People Go

The floor of the cabin felt cold under Harriet's quilt. She saw a weak beam of sunlight on the wall.

"Ummmm." She groaned. Her head hurt. Dizzy. Why was she lying abed when the sun shone through the chinks in the cabin?

"Minty? Honey, it's your mama. Old Rit."

Harriet could only grunt as she felt her mother's hand brush her cheeks. Why did she have that stabbing pain in her head? It hit with every beat of her heart and nearly took her breath away.

"Minty, honey, you been pow'ful sick with that crushin' hole in your head."

*Minty? Was that her name? Who was Harriet?* The drumming of blood beat in her ears. She tried to stay to feel her mother's hand on her face, but she slowly began lifting up again, floating across the fields.

As she flew over the slave quarters, she heard strains of one of her favorite songs:

Oh, freedom. Oh, freedom. Oh, freedom, over me.
And before I be a slave, I'll be buried in my grave,
And go home to my Lord and be free.

Was she dreaming? She could see the overseer in the cornfield below, but he couldn't see her. As she crossed the Big Buckwater River, she wondered if Mr. Cook was checking his trapline. Swim, little muskrats. Swim to freedom. Freedom. That's what flying felt like. Freedom.

She crossed back, looking down on the red bandanas of slaves working in the fields. As she flew higher, a new song began to play in her ears:

Go down, Moses,
Way down in Egypt-land.
Tell ol' Pharaoh
To let My people go.

*Go down.* It felt like a command. *Did Moses wish he could fly away when he was told to go down to Egypt to help his people to freedom?* Harriet felt her body become heavier. Her head began to throb with pain. Lower and lower. How she longed to fly above the plantation again.

She remembered a prayer she prayed long ago, "Lord Jesus, help me be strong for You. Help me to stand when I need to take a stand, to run when You call me to freedom, and to return when You call me back."

"Rit, she's comin' round again." Annie spoke softly.

"Honey-child," said Old Rit, stroking her cheek, "do you know where you be?"

"Uh-huh." She meant to nod her yes, but the pain in her head was intense. "I came back to Egypt-land."

"No, child. This be our own cabin on the Brodas Plantation." Rit turned and spoke to Annie. "She still betwixt wakin' and sleepin'."

"Mebbe she was jes' dreamin', Rit," said Annie as she stood to leave.

"I came back," Harriet whispered.

"God brought you back, Minty. He shorely did." Annie paused in the door. "I'll be back tonight, Rit, so you can get some sleep."

Harriet loved the feel of her mother's hand on her face.

"Do you 'members the corn shuckin' over to the Barrett place?" asked Rit.

"I think so."

"There was a slave fixin' to run and when you refused to help the overseer, he threw a two-pound weight and it purt' near crushed your skull." Rit settled in on the floor next to Harriet to tell her all that had happened since.

Though Harriet drifted in and out of sleep as her mother talked, she understood that she lay near death for many months. Christmas had long since passed without Harriet even knowing.

She raised her hand to her forehead. Over her eye she felt

the swelling and the odd squishiness of her head. As she touched it she heard a whooshing sound in her ears and felt the blackness creep up once again.

"Just lie still, Harriet, and don't be touchin' it. The bone still needs to knit over your brain if it can."

Her mother's voice came from what seemed like a long way away.

"You wakin' up, child?" Annie sat next to her pallet.

"I'm awake."

"You gettin' stronger every day," Annie said.

"Why do I keep fallin' asleep?" Harriet was aware that she often fell into a deep sleep right in the middle of a sentence. Her mother said that when she woke up, she always continued the sentence as if she was never interrupted. She did gain strength every day. Sometimes she even had an hour or two without pain, but the dullness and sleeping attacks continued.

"That doctor Master fetched for you said you goin' have sleepin' fits and headaches the rest of your life. He called it a brain injury."

"You mean I might fall into that sleep anytime, no matter what I'm doing?" Harriet couldn't imagine how she could work anymore. When she had one of those spells, no one was able to rouse her.

"That's right, but don't you be frettin' 'bout it, child." Annie had her no-nonsense voice. "You be thankin' the good Lord for them spells."

*Thank God? Whatever was Annie thinkin'?* All those
months she lay in a coma, Harriet had tasted freedom. How
she wanted to fly away, but she had been called back into her
Egypt-land. She was sure of it. She knew the Lord had given
her the courage to return, but she thought it was because He
wanted a Moses to bring her people into the Promised Land.
If her brain was damaged and if she could fall into a sleeping
spell without warning, what good was she?

"Harriet? You listenin'?"

"Yes, Annie."

"You 'members people trompin' in and out of here when
you was sickest?"

"I think so."

"Know what they was doin'?"

Harriet was tired but she knew Annie wasn't about to let
up. "What were they doing, Annie?"

"Ol' Brodas paraded white folks in here, one after the
other, tryin' to sell you South." The stormy look on Annie's
face left no doubt of her feelings.

"South?" Harriet knew the fear tied up in that one word.

"Master Barrett insist Master Brodas punish you and send
you far away before you make more trouble. But soon as
those speculators poked around a bit, they heard tell 'bout
your spells, and they hightailed it off the plantation." Annie
laughed. "Ever' last one of them!"

"Will they come back?"

"Not likely." Annie laughed again. "Your father heard
Ol' Brodas sayin' that it looks like he's stuck with you again."

"Oh, Annie."

"That's why you need to git down on your knees—well,

not jes' yet—but you need to thank the good Lord for those spells."

Harriet woke up to find her father sitting by her pallet. She knew it must be nighttime.

"I hear you've been frettin' about your spells." Ben always came right to the point.

"Uh-huh."

"Minty-girl, you are blessed to be alive."

"I know, Ben, but I was sure that God wanted me to come back for a special job." Harriet didn't have to explain what she meant by "come back." She had spent long hours telling her father about her dreams. "Now I wonder how I can be like Moses. How can I ask Pharaoh to let my people go?"

"Is that what's worryin' you, child?"

"Yes. I think God wants me to do something—I'm not sure what—but how can I do it now?"

"Did you know that Moses said the very same thing when God asked him to lead the children to the Promised Land?"

"He did?" How come Harriet didn't remember that part of the story?

"Even after God showed His miracles, Moses tried to wiggle out. He said his tongue got all tangled up when he tried to talk. He worried 'bout what ol' Pharoah would say face-to-face with a slow-witted Moses." Ben looked deep into Harriet's eyes. "What do you think God said to Moses?"

"Did He get mad at Moses?"

"No. He asked Moses who made the tongue that got tangled. I think Moses remembered that God doesn't call some-one without givin' him all he needs to do the job. God already planned to give Moses a helper—his brother Aaron."

"I remember now." Harriet also knew what her father was saying to her. Stop worrying about shortcomings.

Harriet knew that when the time was right, she'd be ready—with the help of God. Somewhere off in the distance she heard the start of a song. It started with one clear voice, but one by one others joined in.

> Go down, Moses,
> Way down in Egypt-land.
> Tell ol' Pharaoh
> To let My people go.

After the song died out, Harriet thought about it for a long time. "Lord Jesus, help me be strong for You. Help me to stand when I need to take a stand, to run when You call me to freedom, and to return when You call me back."

# Epilogue

Harriet Tubman has become a legend. In the story, she prays, "Lord Jesus, help me be strong for You. Help me to stand when I need to take a stand, to run when You call me to freedom, and to return when You call me back."

That is exactly what she did. Harriet bravely made her way to freedom, but found God calling her to rescue others. In the story, she often wondered about that mysterious Underground Railroad. Little did she know that she would become its most famous conductor. Eventually called the "Moses of her people," Harriet made the dangerous trip back into the South nineteen times to lead more than 300 slaves to freedom. Despite her sleeping spells, she never "ran her train off the track, nor lost a single passenger."

The events in this book are true, though we can only guess about the actual words that Harriet spoke. We do know that her faith in God was the most important part of her life.

In her own words (written in the style used in her biography by her friend Sarah Bradford):

> "'Pears like, I prayed all de time," she said, "about my work, eberywhere; I was always talking to de Lord. When I went to the horse-trough to wash my face, and took up de water in my hands, I said, 'Oh, Lord, wash me, make me clean.' When I took up de towel to wipe my face and hands, I cried, 'Oh, Lord, for Jesus' sake, wipe away all my sins!' When I took up de broom and began to sweep, I groaned, 'Oh, Lord, whatsoebber sin dere be in my heart, sweep it out, Lord, clar and clean . . .'"

And when someone congratulated her on her bravery, she would always answer, "Don't, I tell you, Missus, 'twan't me, 'twas de Lord! Jes' so long as he wanted to use me, he would take keer of me, an' when he didn't want me no longer, I was ready to go; I always tole him, I'm gwine to hole stiddy on to you, an' you've got to see me trou."

During the Civil War Harriet Tubman worked as a nurse and later a scout for the Union. After the war, she bought a large home in Auburn, New York, with the proceeds from the sale of the Bradford biography and cared for the homeless and the hungry. In her last years she grew vegetables and sold them door-to-door in order to have the money to feed all who came to her door. Upon her death she left her home and her ministry to the church.

# Epilogue

To learn more about the grown-up Harriet Tubman, read:

*Harriet Tubman: The Moses of Her People* by Sarah Bradford
*Harriet Tubman: Conductor on the Underground Railroad* by
    Ann Petry

# Glossary

**Basers.** People who set the handclapping rhythm and guided the melody and harmony of the spiritual singing.

**Basket name.** The name used by slaves in their childhood.

**Card.** A wire-toothed brush used to disentangle fibers such as wool before spinning.

**Caterwauling.** Loud yelling.

**Coffle.** A group of slaves chained together.

**Colicky.** Abdominal pains.

**Hank.** Coil.

**Harnesses.** The frames of a weaver's loom that are moved to create a pattern in the cloth.

**Heddles.** Wires in a weaver's loom that hold the threads used to make cloth.

**Hogsheads.** Large barrels.

**Keening.** Mournful crying.

**Linsey-woolsey.** A coarse fabric made of linen or cotton and wool.

**Pick.** One pass of the *weft* through the *shed* in a weaver's loom.

**Pone.** A cake made of cornmeal.

**Reed.** A comb that separates the *warp* during weaving.

**Ring shout.** A form of worship when a group forms a wide circle and begins a shuffling step around the circle accompanied by their shouting chant to the rhythmic beat of a stick.

**Scullery.** A room used for washing dishes.

**Settee.** A couch.

**Shed.** The opening between *warp* threads where the *weft* passes through.

**Shift.** A dress that was like a long shirt.

**Shot.** One pass of the *weft* through the *shed* in a weaver's loom.

**Sixpence.** A coin worth six English pennies.

**Sticker.** A person who beat the rhythm with a broom handle on a wooden box for a *ring shout*.

**Stone.** Fourteen pounds.

**Switch.** A thin tree branch with whip-like flexibility.

**Tow linen.** Low-quality linen made of short flax fibers.

**Treadles.** Levers pressed by the foot to move the *harnesses* in a weaver's loom.

**Twill.** A diagonal weave in cloth.

**Warp.** The threads on a loom or in fabric that run the length. To *warp* a loom means to string these threads into place so that weaving can begin.

**Wattle and daub.** Reeds or branches woven together and covered with mud to form a structure.

**Weft.** The threads that fill the *warp* to make cloth.

**Winding sheet.** A shroud used for burial.

# Further Insights by Moody Press

## *THE TINKER'S DAUGHTER*

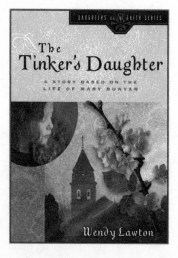

John Bunyan, the author of Pilgrim's Progress, mentions only one of his six children in his memoirs - Mary. Born blind in 1650, her story still intrigues us nearly 350 years later. When her father was imprisoned for unlawful preaching, it was 10-year old Mary who traveled the streets of Bedford each day, brining soup to her father in prison.

Mary developed a fierce determination for independence, after spending years proving that she was not hindered by her blindness. Only when she admitted that she needed help did she turn to the Lord; the Source of all strength.

ISBN: 0-8024-4099-1, Paperback